Enjoy

Shirley Shapiro

Spinning Tales
Shirley Shapiro

Perry Publishing

Copyright © 1996 by Shirley Shapiro and Perry Publishing
Cover photograph copyright © Images 1996 by PhotoDisc, Inc.

Published by Perry Publishing
    5087 Columbia Road
    Columbia, Maryland 21044

All rights reserved. No portion of this book may be reproduced in any form without the prior writted permission of the copyright holders.

Library of Congress Catalog Card Number 96-70170
ISBN 0-9643728-5-1
First printing, November 1996

Printed by Reed Hann
    Williamsport, PA 17701

Table Of Contents

Sour Pickles 5

A Broken Wrist, A Mended Heart 7

Bubba 11

Bubbas & Zadas, Then & Now 14

Cinnamon Buns 17

Dayenu
(It Would Have Been Enough) 23

How To Be A Mensch 25

If Only I Could 27

Never Too Late 29

Passover Memories 31

Rebirth 34

Rosh Hashanna 36

Sunflowers 38

The Golden Medina	41
Treblinka	47
Tsurris	51
Yahrtzeit	55
Giselle	62
The Good Old Days	67
The Partners	71
Six Months	74
Rock Candy	77
The Dilemma	80
Minnie	86

Sour Pickles

I hope he doesn't kiss me today. His beard feels so scratchy on my cheek. I wonder how come so much hair grows on his face and nothing on top of his head?

He must be about a hundred years old. He has so many wrinkles. I can hardly see his eyes because his glasses are so thick. I wonder why he has a wart on the tip of his long nose?

"What can I do for you today, little lady?"

He always calls me little lady.

I stand on my toes and look into the big wooden barrel and point to one of the fat pickles swimming in the water. "I'd like that big one, please."

Mr. Gross reaches in, pulls out a sour pickle and wipes the dripping juices on his apron. When he takes my penny, his hand feels like the old leather chair in our living room.

The grocery store has so many smells. My mouth begins to water. I can almost taste the corned beef and the salamis and lox and smoked fish in the glass counters and the herrings and the sour tomatoes in other wooden barrels next to the sour pickles.

Mr. Gross smiles at me. One of his front teeth is

missing. "Come back soon, little lady." When he kisses my cheek, I smell cigarette smoke.

The bell jingles when I open the door. It makes me think of Tinkerbell in my book about Peter Pan and Wendy. I can read most of the words in that book.

I bite into the pickle. I like the garlicky taste. Some of the juice squirts into my nose and makes me sneeze. I hope none of the juice runs down the new Shirley Temple dress my aunt brought home from the factory.

"It has a second in it," she told me. "So, the boss let me have it."

I never had a new dress that wasn't just for Rosh Hashanna.

I lick the pickle juice off my fingers and skip home. Now that I'm five years old, I can cross the street myself. Maybe tomorrow my Bubba will give me three pennies and I can get a cone of ice cream at the candy store.

A Broken Wrist, A Mended Heart

The cobblestones scraped my arm as I landed on the street. Blood trickled from the slight wound.

Jumping to my feet, I looked around, hoping no one saw me fall, hoping no one would call me a klutz and laugh at me. I sucked the blood from my arm, applied pressure with a handkerchief and continued walking toward the park.

Fairmount Park; the only place in Strawberry Mansion where you could hear the sounds of birds and crickets. The only place you could see trees and grass and flowers. The only place where you could catch a breath of air on a hot summer day.

Fairmount Park wasn't as beautiful in 1937 as it used to be. The statues were chipped, the fountains didn't work anymore, and the gardens looked neglected, but a certain magic still existed.

I climbed the small hill overlooking the Schuylkill River and paused for a moment to catch my breath and check the scrape on my arm. The bleeding stopped, but my wrist throbbed slightly. I flexed it back and forth and moaned in pain.

The mound of grass beneath the large Sycamore

tree felt damp as I settled down, cradled my arm and admonished myself for being so careless. Why does everything happen to me, I wondered.

I leaned my head against the tree and looked up at the white, billowy clouds in the sky. The family said my mother was up in Heaven, but no matter how hard I tried all these years, I couldn't see her. There were red and purple streaks across the blue. My teacher told the class it meant another hot day was on its way.

It didn't matter. Hot or cold, the days were all the same. All sad and lonely. No one cared about me anymore. My father walked around the house like a ghost, never talking, just smoking his cigarettes or sitting and playing solitaire. He wouldn't care if I disappeared. He probably wouldn't even notice.

A mosquito buzzed near me. I brushed it aside and cried out as another pain shot through my arm. Gently, I massaged it, then examined a swelling around my wrist.

Perspiration ran down my body. Goose bumps stood out on my arms. I had to get home!

A hot summer sun burned my skin as I walked down the hill. Kneeling beside a small creek, I splashed water on my face, soaked my handkerchief and pressed it against the swollen, aching wrist.

I thought of Franklin D. Roosevelt's voice booming out through open windows on the tiny streets. At night, every radio tuned in to his "Fireside Chats"; each listener hanging on every word of encouragement. To the people in Strawberry Mansion, FDR was a demi-god.

"Why couldn't he be my father?" I thought. "He would take good care of me."

I climbed the steps to my house and opened the door with my good hand.

"Is that you?" My father's voice was gruff, his accent heavy. He stood in the small foyer, blocking my path.

"What's the matter? You don't feel good?" His hands felt heavy on my shoulders. "You don't feel good?" He repeated. He gasped as he looked at my swollen wrist.

"*Oy, gavult*, we'll go to the Emergency Room. Come, we'll take the trolley.

I sat close to him on the trolley car, my sore hand in my lap, twisting and turning it a little to make certain there was truly a break . . . a break that might mend the rift between my father and me.

The smell of antiseptics in the emergency room, the love and concern on my father's face and the frenzy with which he searched his pockets for the one dollar charge in the hospital, have always remained with me. I remember the tears in his eyes as he watched the cast being put on my wrist. I tried to hide my pleasure as I realized that, although he didn't know how to say the words, my father really loved me. ■

Bubba

She was barely five feet tall. Her wispy hair was pulled back in a bun, held in place with two large combs, barely concealing the large cyst protruding from the back of her head.

Wrinkles furrowed Bubba Golda's face, her eyes reflected the tragedy of having lost a husband and two children.

She placed the woolen shawl on her head and adjusted her glasses. The thick lenses distorted her blue eyes, making them almost disappear.

She struck the match and touched it to the candles in the silver candelabra my sister and I helped her polish.

"Boruch atoh Adonoy, eloheinu melech haolom..." Blessed art thou...

It was the Sabbath and a feeling of peace and serenity filled my Bubba's home.

The house smelled of the Sabbath. The pungent odor of pine soap used to scrub the floors and the walls intermingled with aromas rising from the kitchen. Chicken soup simmered on the stove, freshly baked *challah* and cinnamon buns filled with plump raisins and nuts and encrusted with delicious honey, all combined to etch their way into my soul.

I was six, and painful memories of the past two years were slowly ebbing away; my mother's death, my father's seeming indifference, and the shifting from one place to another were slipping from my consciousness. I basked in the warmth of my Bubba's love. Her arms were a shield of protection about me.

"Asher kidishanu b'mitzva tov, vitzi vanu lahadlik ner, shel Shabbos."

She completed the blessing. *"Gut Shabbos, kinderloch. Gut Shabbos."* She kissed us and held us close.

The sound of the lamplighter broke the spell, as he placed his ladder against the pole and ignited the gas outside our home. A lone star shone in the darkening sky.

In the midst of a world standing on the brink of war, a country wracked with unemployment and indecision, a family torn apart by death and deprivation, thanks to my Bubba, my sweet grandmother, a feeling of peace and security filled my life.

Now I am the grandmother. Not the uneducated, unsophisticated Bubbas I once knew, with oxford shoes and surgical hose and an apron tied around a shapeless waist.

Carefully, I apply my makeup, brush my hair in place and don my best tee shirt, slacks and sneakers as I greet the Sabbath with my family. I pray for the wisdom to instill in my grandchildren the same values my Bubba gave to me.

As I recite the blessings and watch flickering candles cast shadows across the walls, I give thanks to God for the memory of my Bubba and her Sabbath lights.

ה

Bubbas & Zadas, Then & Now

Many, many years ago, when I was a little girl, Jewish grandparents were known as Zadas and Bubbas. They were very, very old people. I don't think they were ever young. In fact, I believe G-d put them on earth at an old age to take care of their children and grandchildren.

Zadas almost always had beards, mustaches and long *payis*. They wore *tsitsis* under their shirts and *yarmulkes* on their heads. The *yarmulkes*, although of religious significance, also helped to hide their bald spots.

Zadas were usually short and chubby with stooped shoulders from studying the Torah or bending over sewing machines to earn a living for the family. They had twinkling eyes and happy faces and false teeth that clicked when they spoke in rapid Yiddish.

During the Zada era, there were grandmothers known as Bubbas; women married to the Zadas.

Most of the Bubbas looked alike, with snow white hair pulled back in buns and held in place with large combs. Their faces were wrinkled and their hands red and coarse from scrubbing, cleaning and cooking day and night. They wore shapeless dresses covered by large, food stained aprons. Their favorite expressions were "*Ess*, my *kind*, people in Europe are starving," and "Don't forget to be a *mensch*."

Todays Bubbas and Zadas have been replaced by imposters. They are known by various aliases: the female species are called Mom-Mom, Grams, Nanny, Voo-Voo, or sometimes even "Sal."

The males are known by other names: Pop-Pop, Bee-Bop, or just plain "Bill."

Some of the impostors dye their hair, wear fancy clothing and jewelry and even have plastic surgery performed to erase any tell-tale signs of age. At times they look even younger than their own children. This can lead to a great deal of confusion.

These modern day Bubbas and Zadas dance at discos, drive their own cars, belong to country clubs, exercise to keep fit, travel around the world and are up on the latest books, plays, movies and world events.

They play tennis, golf, canasta and Mah Jongg. Some of the females even have the temerity to go to the beach in sexy bikinis. And would you believe it, these modern day Bubbas and Zadas are still romantically involved with each other.

There are some things that remain constant. No matter what they are called, there is nothing to equal the love and pride of grandparents for grandchildren. They are there when needed, shed tears of joy at Bar and Bat Mitzvahs, pray to see their grandchildren walk down the aisle at their wedding, and in between, kiss away fears and tears.

Whatever you call them; Bubba, Zada, Mom-Mom or Pop-Pop, they spell love and they will still tell you "Finish your food, people in Europe are starving," and "don't forget to be a *mensch*.

Cinnamon Buns

Sylvia hugged her arms close to her body to ward off cold air penetrating her thin coat. She pressed her face against the bakery window and, almost smelling the cinnamon buns displayed on the shelf, remembered the buns her Buba Golda used to bake every Friday, along with the braided Sabbath challahs.

Sylvia fingered the two pennies in her coat pocket; the two pennies she found in the cloak room at her elementary school. Not enough to buy one of the luscious cakes in the window. Besides, her conscience bothered her for not turning the money in to the teacher.

A chill ran through her as the air turned cooler. She moved closer to the walls of the building to absorb some of the warmth coming through the bricks. Frustrated, she turned toward home, trying to ignore the hungry rumbling in her stomach.

The mailman climbed the steps to her front door. In spite of snowflakes falling on her face, her cheeks burned with shame. She prayed no one would see the relief check the mailman was delivering.

"Why?" Sylvia asked herself. "Why does everything have to be so rotten?"

Her Buba Fayga's asthmatic wheezing greeted her

as she entered the house. Sylvia winced as she heard the familiar spitting into the paper bag. The sound repulsed her, then made her ashamed of her feelings.

"Sylvia, is that you? What took you so long to come home from school? Suppose we needed you for something?" Her Buba's voice trailed off as another coughing spell overtook her.

Sylvia ignored her grandmother's question. She had learned that home was not a place where people communicated. Everyone retreated into a private world of silence. She was only ten years old, but she had learned her lesson well.

Her father sat in the living room, his crutches propped near his chair, eyes staring vacantly out at the snow which now swirled even faster.

"How do you feel?" she mumbled through stiff lips. She fought the urge to walk near, touch him, tell him she was sorry he seemed to have so much pain.

"How do you feel?" she asked again. There was no response. Just a small shrug of his shoulders as he continued to stare at the falling snow.

Sylvia walked upstairs to her bedroom and closed the door behind her. The house felt as cold as the outdoors. "Maybe the coal is gone," she thought. "Maybe we'll all get sick and die and then we won't have to worry about anything anymore."

A shiver ran through her. "God forgive me for all my wicked thoughts," she said aloud. She opened a drawer and took out a pad and pencil and wrote;

January 16, 1937. Dear Diary, today is another cold, rotten day, just like all the other days. Why does it have to be this way? I miss my other Buba so much. Why did she have to die, too? Why does everyone have to die?

She put the pencil down and walked to the window. Thoughts of her mother's death followed by the loss of her grandmother were too much for her to bear. She watched the snow fall faster, the light layer sticking to the sidewalks.

Sylvia sighed as she remembered the day she and her sister were taken to Buba Golda's house. It was a day like today; cold and snowy and miserable.

She was only five years old and frightened. She held tightly to her father's hand as they stood at her grandmother's door. She wondered if her sister was scared, too, but she wouldn't ask.

Sweet smells struck her as they entered the house. On the dining room table, next to the silver candlesticks were two loaves of challah and a platter of cinnamon buns; the rich, gooey topping still warm and bubbling.

"Come, little darlings, I'll give you milk and warm

cinnamon buns as soon as we put your things away. Would you like that?"

Sylvia nodded, the cold knot in her chest slowly melting. By the time she looked around, her father was gone.

In the early light of dawn, as snow covered the streets, muffling the sound of the milkman's horse and wagon, Sylvia slept contentedly next to her grandmother's warmth. It was the first time she felt safe since her mother's death.

That was five years ago. So much had happened since then.

Sylvia picked the pencil up again.

Why couldn't it last? It was so nice with Buba Golda. I felt so safe.

She smiled as she replaced bitter memories with happy thoughts; playing in the park with her cousins and her sister, the sweet smell of clover in the air and butterflies flapping beautiful wings against the blue sky. There were picnics and rides to a country fair and the taste of freshly picked corn drenched in butter.

Now, her father's footsteps shuffling up the stairs broke her reverie. The slow, deliberate steps; the clip-clop of his crutches were an assault to her ears. Once more, her conscience burned. Never would she allow anyone to know her thoughts, not even her sister. She would never open up to another soul. She would remain silent forever.

Sylvia put the pad and pencil back in the drawer and walked to the window. Snow fell faster, now sticking to sidewalks where children scampered in the thin white blanket.

Sylvia sighed. For the rest of her life, she would keep all her feelings to herself.

"No!" Buba Golda's voice came back to her. "Don't keep everything tied up inside you. It's not good. Try to talk about your feelings. It will be better for you."

THE WOMAN WALKED BRISKLY DOWN SNOW FILLED STREETS. She wrapped her fur collar closer to her face, stopped at the bakery, pulled the door open and inhaled the aroma of freshly baked cinnamon buns.

"The usual?" the woman behind the counter asked.

"Of course." She looked at her watch. It was 8:15AM, just enough time to get to the studio and have her cinnamon buns and coffee before the show.

"How do you find so much to talk about every morning?" the clerk asked. "You never seem to run out of subjects."

"That's why they call it "Talk With Sylvia," she

answered. "And don't tell anyone, but it's your cinnamon buns that inspire me every day."

Dayenu
(It Would Have Been Enough)

The hotel dining room sparkles with lights from huge crystal chandeliers. Crisp white cloths cover dozens of round tables. Each table contains a platter with symbols of the Passover seder; a roasted egg, a roasted shank bone, parsley, bitter herbs, salt water and a mixture of chopped apples, nuts, cinnamon and wine. Each item is a vital part of the re-telling of the Exodus from Egypt.

I sit among hundreds of Passover guests and imagine myself in Egypt thousands of years ago.

I am an ancient Hebrew maiden. The sun beats down on my darkened skin as I mix mortar for building of the pyramids. My back and arms ache. I run my tongue across dry, parched lips, longing for water, but I dare not pause. The sting of whip is still fresh; the whip of Egyptian soldiers who watch our every move.

There is no hope. We are all doomed to a life of slavery; our children, grandchildren and all the generations to follow.

But wait! There is talk of a man among us who will lead us from bondage. They say his name is Moses. Do we dare to believe?

Now I am at the edge of the Red Sea. Angry waters lap against my ankles, but I hardly notice. Fear overcomes me as I waver between death by drowning or capture by soldiers close behind.

Suddenly, the sea parts and my people and I are led to freedom.

"Dayenu," we shout. "Dayenu."

I shake my head. I'm back in the dining room, but the sound of "Dayenu" echoes in my ears. The guests are singing "Dayenu" loud and clear.

"Dayenu" for so many things. For delivering us from slavery in Egypt, for rescuing us from tyrants who have attempted genocide against us, and Crusaders and Inquisitors who have tried to convert us.

I look at the wrinkled, time-worn faces around me and see a glow of love, a feeling of belonging in the myopic, faded eyes. There are tattoos on some of the shriveled arms; arms that have withstood untold tortures; arms that continue to embrace the beloved Torah despite so many obstacles.

I recite the blessing over the matzo, the bread of affliction, then join my people in singing "Dayenu."

Thank you, G-d, for all your blessings.

"Dayenu." ה

How To Be A Mensch

First, in order to learn how to be a *mensch*, it is vital that you know the meaning of the word.

Mensch; translated literally from Yiddish, means "Person." But the broader translation is "a caring, benevolent human being."

Now we can proceed.

Rule number 1........ Be tactful. Be considerate of the feelings of others. When your friend shows you a picture of her new grandchild and you think it is a really ugly baby, DON'T, I repeat, DON'T burst out laughing. Instead, look her in the eye, smile and say, "Now, that is really a baby."

Rule number 2........ Be encouraging. When your favorite nephew drives by to show off his new two-door Mazda convertible, make him feel good. Tell him you hope business will pick up and maybe next year he can afford a four-door car with a roof.

Rule number 3........ Be generous. When your best friend decides to diet to try to lose the three hundred excess pounds she has put on, don't bake some of her favorite chocolate cookies and insist that she finish every one of them. Don't tell her it will give her the strength to go on.

Rule number 4..... Be undemanding. When you buy your daughter two dresses, a red one and a blue one and she comes out wearing the blue dress, don't look at her sadly and say, "What's the matter? Didn't you like the red dress?"

Rule number 5..... Be tolerant. If your son, daughter or grandchild brings a romantic interest to your door, accept him or her for what they are. Disregard the unkempt, dirty, uncouth appearance. Just smile politely and excuse yourself. Go to your kitchen and put your head in the oven. Hopefully, you don't have an all-electric home.

Follow these rules and you will become a full fledged *mensch*.

If Only I Could

If only I could...and I can.. I will close my eyes and let my imagination carry me to other places, other identities, other lives. I will travel near and far and taste of worlds I've only read about.

I count to three...and I am transported to Vienna. It is the nineteenth century. Strains of Strauss waltzes reach out to me. My gold slippered feet move in rhythm as I dance in the arms of handsome admirers. I am young and beautiful. My blond hair, piled high on my head, is interlaced with gems that sparkle under the shimmering crystal chandeliers in the vast ballroom. My brocaded gown bows and curtsies with each graceful movement of my slim body. I lower my long lashes demurely and blush as my partners tell me of my loveliness. The world is mine to conquer.

If only I could...and I can...I count to three again, and now I am an Indian maiden sitting beside a river bank. My skin is tanned by the bright rays of the warm summer sun. My hair is long and straight and shiny black. My dark eyes, as dark as a midnight sky, drink in the wonders of my beautiful land; the clear blue heavens above me, the tall, majestic trees swaying in the slight breeze, and graceful animals prancing freely across rich green grass. I put my bare feet in the rippling water and feel it tickle my toes. I throw my head back and laugh and the sound floats through the air and into the thick woods behind me.

If only I could. . .and I can. . .I will count to three again. Now I am omnipotent. I will undo all the evils of the world. I will rid the world of the scourge -- especially the innocent infants and children afflicted with AIDS and born addicted to crack. I will give them an opportunity to taste the beauties of life, to have their dreams and fantasies. I will take away the hunger and pain and fear all around the world . .the bellies distended from malnutrition, the spindly arms and legs, the bulging eyes searching, pleading for help.

I will awaken from their graves millions of people murdered by madmen seeking to dominate the world; especially children cut down in Iraq, in Africa, in Sudan.

I will wave my magic wand and call back to life the millions of victims; especially the million and a half children incinerated by Nazis. I will say, "Rise and live again. Take your rightful place in society. Maybe you will be the scientist who will find a cure for Cancer, AIDS, Heart Disease, or the musician whose music can now be heard. You will bring forth future generations who will perpetuate your faith, the faith that gave birth to two other major religions. Come and live again. Reclaim the birthright that is yours. "

Oh, if only I could.

Never Too Late

The pain was constant. Intense, unbearable pain. It enveloped his entire body. His feet jutted out from the sheet on his hospital bed. He heard the doctor whisper, "gangrene" and he saw the nurse cringe as she averted her eyes from the blackened toes and turned from the offensive odor.

Tears gathered in the corners of Herman's eyes. His life was coming to an end and there were still so many things he wanted to do, places he wanted to see, and things he wished he could say to Sylvia.

Sylvia, the daughter he had been so neglectful of for so many years. Now it was too late to make amends.

She sat by his bedside, her small, slim hand resting gently on his arm. She couldn't know that the slightest pressure on his disease-racked body produced terrible pain, but he wouldn't shake her hand away. Too many years had passed without any physical or social contact between them.

Herman ran his tongue across his dry lips. His lungs were about to burst...he had to get air. He strained against the oxygen mask, but there was no relief.

He turned his head toward his daughter and tried to form words. He wanted to tell her he loved her, ask her to forgive him for not being a better father, try to explain why he had walked out so many years ago. He had no voice.

Shadows danced on the stark white walls of his hospital room. He saw himself as a small boy again, walking through deep snow-filled lanes in Russia. His feet were whole again. Cold winds swirled against his face and bit into his cheeks. He heard the whinny of Cossack's horses in the distance. His parents, long dead, appeared before him, beckoning, smiling, "Come to us. We'll protect you," they said.

He turned his head back to the wall. He didn't want Sylvia to see the tears which now ran freely.

"I love you, Sylvia." The words swirled around and around in his head, but he couldn't say them aloud. "Forgive me for everything. I love you."

She leaned forward and kissed his cheek. Her lips felt cool against his feverish, unshaven face. Gently, silently, she stroked his head.

"I know, I know," she whispered. "I love you, too."

Suddenly, his pain was gone. "She heard me," he thought. "She heard me."

Darkness dissolved into a bright, glowing light as he reached up to grasp his parents' waiting hands.

Passover Memories

We scampered across the vacant lot, my cousins, sisters and I. Memories still warm me like the sun that shone down on us that day.

Smell of clover was strong, new life sprouted on Sycamore trees and multi-colored butterflies fluttered above our heads. Cold winter snows lay buried and forgotten as spring burst forth once more.

A huckster led his horse and wagon through the narrow street. His husky voice shouted above our childish laughter. "Fresh fruit, fresh vegetables. Horseradish for your seder plate. Come and get it!"

I paused to watch my grandmother come out to make her purchase, her coins wrapped in a handkerchief in her apron pocket.

She brushed her white hair from her wrinkled face and squinted into the sun. I waved to her, then ran back to play. Her voice followed me. "Come home soon. We need help to get ready for Pesach."

My cousins carried the Passover dishes from the cellar. My sisters and I helped chop apples and nuts for the seder plate.

Strong holiday smells surrounded us; my grandmother's sweet cherry wine, her fluffy matzo balls floating in a kettle of simmering chicken soup and sponge cake rising in the oven next to a pan of potato kugel. I cringed a little as I watched my grandmother chop the gefilte fish and realized it was the carp which swam in our bathtub for several days.

That was over sixty years ago. Although many things have changed, some things remain constant. We still drink wine, but it is bottled by Mogen David. My gefilte fish won't swim in my tub, it will come from a jar and horseradish will be bought at the supermarket, but the symbols on the seder plate will be the same.

The roasted egg and the shankbone to remind us of the Pascal sacrifices. Horseradish, to recall the bitter years of slavery. A mixture of apples, nuts, cinnamon and wine to remember the mortar used to build the pyramids. Salt water to symbolize the tears we shed as slaves. Matzo, the bread of affliction, and parsley to commemorate the festival of spring.

As I prepare for my Passover seder, I drink from the well of early childhood memories.

I see my grandfather at the head of the table, reclining on a pillow as he retells the story of the Exodus from Egypt; the parting of the Red Sea that led us to freedom. I taste my grandmother's tsimmes and compote. But above all, I feel love and security that lifted us above problems of a depression stricken world poised on the brink of war.

"Please, God," I will pray as I light my holiday candles, "Help me to build strong memories for my children and grandchildren, so they, in turn, will never forget their heritage as they welcome in our beautiful festival of spring."

ח

Rebirth

Small, green leaves sprouted on the remaining trees in our yard. Rebirth...after the fury unleashed by Hurricane Andrew.

Rebirth. I thought of it as I sat in my temple, ushering in the New Year.

The rich baritone voice of the Cantor blended in perfect harmony with the choir as they chanted songs of hope and faith. The Rabbi's sermon echoed through the sanctuary; a stilling message of deep belief in a Higher Power. The shrill blasting of the Shofar (Ram's Horn) issued a prayer for peace throughout the world.

My mind traveled back many years, and once again I was a small child sitting in a tiny, drab synagogue with my grandmother, listening to the same prayers, the same blasting of the Shofar.

The setting had changed, but the same feeling of love and awe filled my heart that day as it did so long ago.

I watched three generations approach the Holy Ark. The Torah was handed down from father, to son to grandson. One generation to another.

Tradition! A continuity of our faith.

I thought with deep love and emotion of my dear children and grandchildren and prayed that the tradition will live on through them and those to follow.

For a moment, I closed my eyes and said another prayer...a prayer of thanks to the Almighty for seeing us through that night of terror: August 24, 1992, when Hurricane Andrew visited our Miami home.

As the Cantor and choir reached a crescendo, singing praises to G-d and beseeching Him for a brighter tomorrow, I thought again of the new leaves sprouting on my trees.

In my heart, I knew that G-d in His infinite wisdom, always sends healing after a storm. ח

Rosh Hashanna

I sat on a hard wooden bench on the balcony of the Shul, my tiny body sandwiched among the female worshippers.

Below, the Rabbi, his head and body covered with a large prayer shawl, chanted the High Holy day liturgy. His shrill voice bounced off the concrete walls of the tiny sanctuary. I watched the men and boys leaning over the Torah, their bodies swaying back and forth as they recited the prayers, their feet scraping along the sawdust floors.

Rosh Hashana, 1934. The country was deep in depression, trying to recover from the stock market crash, praying for survival under the leadership of Franklin Delano Roosevelt.

The Hebrew words in the prayer books were unfamiliar to me. I was still struggling to learn English. But the feeling of peace and security surrounding me in that drab atmosphere went far beyond reading of the text.

I stole a glance at my grandmother. A knitted shawl covered her white hair, her face a maze of wrinkles, her lips a grim line. But her eyes gripped my attention. In spite of my youth, I recognized a value and belief that has sustained me throughout my life.

Her eyes reflected memories of her own childhood; the many hardships she and her family endured in their native Russia; the pogroms, poverty, and finally the long awaited search for a better life in America, the Goldena Medina. I sensed her belief that it truly awaited.

I saw something else in my grandmother's eyes that holy day; generations who had lived before her and the many generations to follow.

As the Shofar sounded, issuing a call for a new year of good health and peace on earth, my grandmother took my hand. Her own hand felt rough and callused against my smooth skin, but it was a good feeling.

Today, I sit beside *my* husband in a beautiful, modern sanctuary on Rosh Hashana. Stained glass windows send prisms of colored lights throughout the building. I relax on a plush seat against the background of a full choir. Large floral arrangements of daisies and chrysanthemums and Birds of Paradise adorn the carpeted altar.

In spite of the many changes that have taken place over the years, some things remain constant.

When I hear the shrill blast of the Shofar, I remember my grandmother and all who came before her.

Shalom. May the New Year bring peace to the entire world. ח

Sunflowers

A sweet smell of clover hung in the air. In the center of the vacant lot, spindly vines twisted together, inching their way to the base of a lone tree. The Sycamore was in full bloom, its leafy branches spread in pride.

Leah and her mother sat on a blanket beneath the tree, their faces turned toward the summer sun. Ruth sang softly as she stroked her daughter's hair.

"Lu, lu, lu, lu, lu, hush a bye. Dream of the angels way up high. Lu, lu, lu, lu, lu, don't you cry. Momma won't go away."

Leah loved the sound of her mother's voice. It made her feel good inside. She sighed and snuggled closer.

She was so glad her mother was back. She didn't like it when she was away. She was in the hospital, they said. She'll come home soon. . .as soon as she gets better.

Well, now she was better and Leah didn't want her to ever go away again.

"Sleep in my arms while you still can, childhood is but a day. Even when you're a big woman, Momma won't go away."

Ruth finished the song. "Come, let's take a walk around the lot and see if there are any sunflowers in bloom."

Bright colored butterflies fluttered above them. Bumblebees buzzed among the clover. In a far corner, young boys played baseball with sawed off broomsticks.

"They mashed the sunflowers, Mommy." Leah's lips quivered as she spoke. "The flowers are dead." A tear ran down her cheek and into her mouth. "Those boys are bad. They deaded the pretty sunflowers."

"They didn't mean it, Sweetheart. Don't you worry. The flowers might look dead now, but as long as the roots are still there, new flowers will grow again. God always sends new life. Come, let's go back to our tree, and I'll sing to you again."

Leah moved close to her mother on the blanket and leaned her head against her mother's chest. Something felt funny. She put her hand to the spot where her mother used to be round and soft. The roundness was missing. She touched the other side. That roundness was still there.

Something was wrong!

Leah looked at the tears running down her mother's face. She felt frightened, but didn't really know why.

"Sing the song again, Mommy. Please sing the song to me again.

More than two years passed. Leah walked through the lot on her way to school. She was six years old. Not a baby anymore.

"Momma went to live with God," the family told her.

The grass on the lot was dry and brown, but the few remaining leaves on the Sycamore tree were still bright red and orange.

Leah kicked at the leaves scattered on the ground. She wondered if the boys still played baseball where sunflowers had once grown.

She walked to the corner of the lot.

There, among the twisted clover leaves and dying grass, a beautiful new sunflower stood straight and tall, a butterfly perched on its bright yellow petals.

Leah smiled, lifted her little chin and walked to school.

The Golden Medina

Yussel draped his tallis across his shoulders, recited the blessing and entered the sanctuary. Today was *Rosh Kodesh*, the start of a new month. The service would be a little longer than usual, but he didn't mind. He looked forward to Shabbat; the chanting of the Cantor, the Rabbi's sermon, the mingling with his fellow Jews.

Sunlight filtered through the stained glass windows, scattering colored prisms around the room. Yussel slid into his seat and opened his prayer book as the Cantor began to chant the *Shochen Ahd*.

Yussel smiled as the sweet voice echoed through the sanctuary. He leaned back against his seat, listening to the chanting, feeling an inner peace that always washed over him in shul.

Life has been good, he thought. I have so much to be grateful for. God has been kind.

It wasn't always that way. The early 1930's were difficult times. America was far from the promise of a "*Goldena Medina*" everyone had expected. Who ever thought men would be selling apples on street corners? Who expected a depression that would cripple the economy for so long? This was supposed to be the golden land, the land of opportunity.

Yussel closed his eyes for a few seconds and thought back to the day that marked a change in his life.

He shuffled toward the trolley that day as the sun rose over the small brick houses. His head hung low, his shoulders slouched, his eyes cast downward.

Yussel had been in the country ten years. Nothing was going right. He was thirty years old with a wife who nagged day and night, three children he could barely feed and a job he hated but couldn't leave because there was nothing else available.

Rough cobblestones cut through the hole in his shoe and chafed his foot as he walked.

"America, the *Goldena Medina*," he muttered under his breath. "The land where streets are paved with gold. Feh!" He spat on a rotting watermelon rind lying at the curb. "All I find here are stones that cut through the cardboard in my shoes."

Today would be another burning hot day, a day that would be torture in the factory. No air, no windows, just sweaty, smelly workers bending over sewing machines while the cloth slipped away from their wet hands.

"Feh!" he repeated. He spat again.

"Mister, Mister!" Yussel turned toward the sound of the voice.

Me?" He looked around, then pointed to himself. "Me?" he asked again.

"Yeah. We need you to be the tenth man so we can have our morning *minyan* service."

Yussel laughed. "You want me to help you pray? Find someone else. I don't go to shul anymore. I wouldn't even know how to say the prayers."

"Please, Mister. We need you. Please, it will be a *mitzvah*. Don't worry, the prayers will come back to you. Some things you never forget." The man grabbed Yussel's arm.

Yussel shrugged his shoulders. "Okay, okay. But just this once."

He stepped into the vestibule of the little synagogue and put a *yarmulke* on his head. He took a *tallis* from a hook and draped it around his shoulders. Fingering the silk tassels hanging from the prayer shawl, the long forgotten blessing rushed back to him.

"*Boruch Atoh Adonoy, Eloheinu Melech Ha'olom Asher Kidishanu B'Mitzvosov Vitzivanu Lahisataif B'tsitsis.*"

Yussel stumbled into the small chapel. His worn shoes kicked at the sawdust on the floor. He squinted at the bare concrete walls, the few chairs set around a slightly raised platform.

Eight bearded men formed a circle around the short, frail Rabbi whose head and body were completely covered with a prayer shawl. He swayed back and forth and chanted in a sing-songy nasal tone.

The prayer book felt heavy in Yussel's hand and the *yarmulke* and *tallis* were lead weights on his head and shoulders. His chest and armpits turned wet.

This was his first time in a synagogue since leaving his native Poland.

Poland! How could he forget! Back in a tiny shul with his father. He remembered his awe as he listened to his father recite the daily blessings. Once again, he saw the pride in his father's eyes as he placed a *tallis* around Yussel's shoulders on his *Bar Mitzvah* day. He salivated as he remembered the taste of herring and gefilte fish his mother made for the celebration.

His father and mother. He hadn't thought much about either of them in a long time. They were shadowy figures standing at the dock, wringing their hands and crying as they watched him leave for the *Goldena Medina*.

"*Forgess nisht as du bist a Yid, Yussel,*" his father's rough beard scratched his cheek as he kissed him.

Now, as he sat in shul, he felt the kiss on his cheek again. He shivered. In spite of the heat in the chapel, the chill of icy winters in his village, frost biting through his clothes returned to him. He pulled the prayer shawl closer to ward off the memory.

The Rabbi stood before him. "You'll come again?" he asked.

Yussel stared at the bearded face, the dark, deep-set eyes behind rimless glasses, the long, sharp nose above a bushy gray mustache. It was his father staring at him, his father's eyes piercing through him. He heard his father's voice reminding him to be strong, have faith, be loyal, to never forget his heritage.

"You'll come back?" the Rabbi asked again.

"I'll come back. I'll come back." Yussel answered.

The Rabbi put his hands on Yussel's shoulders and the warmth penetrated his shirt. He thought again of his *Bar Mitzvah* day and the love of his parents. He made a silent vow to save enough money to bring them to America, and another vow to manage to build a better life for his family.

"Bless you," the Rabbi said. "Bless you and your family. May God watch over you and keep you all safe and well."

Yussel stepped out of the synagogue and walked toward the trolley car. His shoe scraped against metal objects glittering under the hot sun. He picked them up and smiled.

"Silver coins," he said to himself. "So, maybe this isn't a "*Goldena Medina*." Maybe the streets aren't lined with gold, but who knows? Silver is also not too bad."

He squared his shoulders and hurried to the trolley car.

Yussel smiled as he watched the ark being opened. Just like an old man to reminisce during *Shabbat* services. Well, there are worse things in life.

His smile grew broader as his son moved toward the podium, preparing to deliver the *Shabbat* sermon. Yussel felt the same pride that welled inside him every week as he "*shepped nachas*" from his son, the Rabbi.

Rabbi Winer cleared his throat, nodded to his father, adjusted the tallis given to him by the little Rabbi in the shul with the sawdust floors and began to speak.

"*Hemshech*." he said, "Tradition. The continuity of our faith. A faith handed down from generation to generation. We shall survive. In spite of every foe that has tried to destroy us, God has sustained us."

Yussel wrapped his own *tallis* closer. Life was good. Yes, it was very good. Thank God for taking us out of Poland and directing us to this "*Goldena Medina*."

He relaxed on his seat and listened intently to the rest of the sermon.

Treblinka

Half a century had passed since the horror of Treblinka. Fifty years, and the smell of rotting flesh and burning bodies. Fifty years, and agonizing screams still echoed in his ears.

Not a second of his life remained free of memories, but, thankfully, it would soon be over. Soon the torment would cease and he could rest in peace beneath the cool, moist ground. He welcomed the end to this tortured existence.

He wrapped his arms around his body to still the trembling as he eased himself off the bed. The loud beat of his heart overpowered the tick of the alarm clock. Time was running out. Running out for him and all others who shared his nightmares.

Slipping callused feet into slippers, he walked slowly to the open window. Faint moonlight shone through vertical blinds that clicked softly together.

Like the rattling of bones, he thought. Bones stacked on top of each other. Bones almost reaching the ceiling. Bones that had once supported living, breathing human beings.

Damn it. It was so long ago, but he couldn't erase the thoughts. They were driving him mad, pursuing him relentlessly. He couldn't eat, sleep or function like a normal person.

Normal Person? Who could be normal after Treblinka?

A dog howled at the street corner. Like the mournful wailing of Treblinka victims. Constant, pleading wailing. The cries of babies torn from mothers' arms, screams of parents, husbands, wives, sisters and brothers. He covered his ears to drown out the sounds, but they never stopped. Their voices built to a terrifying crescendo, slowly making him insane.

Was it the same for the others who were at the death camp? Were they as possessed or did they manage to put the horrors behind them?

He closed the window to shut out the sound of the dog, the rattling of the blinds. If only he could shut out the memories that easily!

A small light shone in the den. He kept it on each night in hopes of stilling his fears. Darkness frightened him. Shadows on the walls stalked him, creaking floorboards screamed at him.

He walked slowly into the den, looking over his shoulder for hidden enemies. His lips felt dry, his throat constricted as he reached up on the shelf for a photo album.

He turned each page with withered, mottled hands that trembled out of control. Soon, the torture would be over. Soon all the people from Treblinka would be gone and the world could forget all that had happened there.

A sharp pain pierced his chest, radiating up to his throat then down through his left arm. The pain grew, invading his entire body. His heart was exploding. He reached for a nitro, then paused and threw the pills on the floor, scattering them on the white tiles.

No more pills. It was time to be free. Free of memories of the last fifty years. Time to join his ancestors and find a long-awaited release from this torture; to finally rest beneath the cool, moist ground.

He slumped forward in the chair. His head struck the table. His eyes rolled upward as he waited anxiously for the Angel of Death to finally bring peace. One withered hand rested on a picture in the album. A picture he, himself, had taken so many years ago. A picture of a Jew in striped prison garb about to join his family in the gas chamber.

The prisoner's voice still haunted him as it had day and night all these years. It was as loud now as it had been that day.

"Nazi bastard," the Jew had shouted. "My last prayer is that you will spend the rest of your days tortured by the memory of what your kind has done. May you never enjoy a peaceful moment for the rest of your life.

And when the Angel of Death comes for you, may you rot in hell for all of eternity, never, ever resting in peace."

ה

Tsurris

Sadie missed calling the eight crack. Bertha declared Mah Jongg on the next tile.

"I bet on you, Sadie," Jenny said in disgust. "I can't believe you let the eight crack go by. Remind me never to bet on you again. Your mind is a million miles away. "

Sadie's eyes watered. "I'm sorry," she said. "It's just that I have so much *tsurris*, I can't concentrate.

"Come, let's break for coffee. Ruth pushed her chair from the table and walked to the kitchen. "Go, sit in the dining room while I cut up the Entenmann's cake. It's fat free. You won't have to worry about cholesterol. And there's only a hundred calories in each slice. Go, sit and make yourselves comfortable."

Molly fidgeted as she fingered the sterling silver fork. She looked at the beautiful Rosenthal china plate in front of her, the crystal water goblet, the linen napkin, beautiful Lladro figures displayed in the large breakfront. She touched the small *Mogen David* around her neck and silently compared it to the diamonds on the other women.

She felt out of place. This was her first Mah Jongg game with Sadie, Jenny, Ruth and Bertha who had been playing together for thirty years. They had invited her to be their fifth, because Tillie, (G-d rest her soul) had passed away suddenly while shopping at Bloomingdales during a storewide clearance.

"*Nu*, Sadie, would you like to share your problems with us? After all, what are friends for if not to share the good and the bad?" Bertha turned to the others who nodded in agreement.

"It's the usual problem nowadays. My grandson, Richie, is going with a *shiksa*." A small sob escaped Sadie's lips. "Not that she's not a lovely girl, G-d forbid, but what's going to become of us if the intermarriage rate keeps increasing? Why can't the young people realize how important it is to perpetuate our faith?"

Bertha laughed. "That's your *tsurris*? Look, as long as they'll be happy, you should count your blessings."

"Count my blessings? That's easy for you to say. My mother's whole family died in Auschwitz. And how do you think my Buba and Zada, they should rest in peace, would feel? They would probably turn over in their graves. I know they wouldn't tell me to count my blessings." She dabbed at her eyes with the tip of her lace handkerchief.

Molly put a comforting hand on Sadie's quivering shoulders. "Have you discussed your feelings with your Rabbi, Sadie?" she asked.

"What Rabbi? Herman and I dropped out of the Temple right after my son's *Bar Mitzvah*. We had no need for a Temple after that. Besides, they raised the dues, and with all our other expenses: the Country Club, Theater Guild, season tickets to the Dolphins games and now the Heat and the Marlins and the Panthers, who can afford to belong to a Temple? But believe me, with or without a Temple, we know we're Jewish in our hearts. My son, Joe was *Bar Mitzvahed* and so was his son, Richie. We always did the right thing."

"It's too bad you didn't live here when Joe was *Bar Mitzvahed*," Jenny said to Molly. "It was the affair of the century. *Oy*, I'll never forget the shrimp they served at the reception that night. They were as big as my hand. My mouth waters when I think of them."

"A lot of good it does to give them a Jewish background. " Sadie sniffed back the tears. "Once they grow up, they do what they want anyway. "

"Why don't you invite the young lady to your home for a *Shabbat* dinner?" Molly suggested. "The candles, the *kiddush*, the blessing over the challah are such beautiful traditions. Maybe she'll decide to convert."

"That would be a wonderful idea, but Friday night we all go to the Country Club for dancing. First, we meet at Woo Ching's for spare ribs and lobster chow mein, and then we work off all the calories. In fact, we were planning to ask you and your husband to join us."

"Thank you, but we don't eat non-kosher food. Besides, Friday night is special to us. Our children and grandchildren come for dinner every *Shabbat*. My little Rachel helps me light the *Shabbat* candles and my grandson, Adam helps his Zada make the *kiddush* and the blessing over the challahs. Then we go to services. I *kvell* when I hear Adam and Rachel sing "*Sholem Aleichem*". It takes me back to my own childhood and all the generations before me. In some small way, I am trying to keep the spirit alive."

Through the beveled glass mirror on the dining room wall, Molly saw the looks exchanged among the four women. She knew without a doubt this would be the last time she would be invited to join their game. She saw the diamonds sparkling on their fingers as they reached for their slice of Entenmann's cake. She smiled to herself. She knew she had riches they would never imagine.

Sadie broke the silence around them. "I guess you think all of that will guarantee your family against intermarrying?"

There are no guarantees," Molly answered. "All I know is, it certainly can't hurt." ח

Yahrtzeit

Ida heard Morris' muffled cries through the thin walls of her condo apartment. Sometimes she heard him talking to his dead wife.

She never knew his wife. She died a few months before Ida moved in to the building, but the other tenants always talked about what a devoted couple they had been.

Ida knew about devotion. After all, she and Albert had a wonderful life together, too. He was gone almost three years, but he was never far from her mind. Moving to Miami Beach, away from the children, away from constant reminders was her first step toward recovery.

She noticed Morris the first day she went to the pool. Something about him reminded her of Albert. Maybe it was the way he stood, his shoulders pushed back proudly, or maybe it was something in his eyes or the way he smiled and thanked her when she brought him chicken soup and matzo balls on Friday night.

There was sadness about him she recognized as a reflection of her own feelings. When she heard the sobs through the wall, she wished she could comfort him in some way. Maybe the chicken soup and matzo balls would help.

Ida saw him buying the yarhtzeit candle and knew that the anniversary of his wife's death was close at hand.

The sight of the little yahrtzeit glass reminded her of the depression years when yahrtzeit or even empty jelly glasses became part of a matched set along with the dishes given out at movie houses each Tuesday night; free with your ten-cent admission. If one broke during the movie, the management rushed over with a replacement.

What a long way we've come, she thought as she pictured the fine sterling and china in the breakfront in her condo, but not a long enough way to help a woman her age overcome the reluctance to make the first move with a man.

She would love to invite him to dinner in her apartment, or ask him to accompany her to one of the condo dances or one of the shows they sponsored, but her early upbringing inhibited her. The most she could bring herself to do was take him the soup and knaidlach.

As she stood behind him in the supermarket line, he pointed to the yahrtzeit glass. "It's for my wife," he said. His eyes were misty behind his glasses. "It will be a year."

Ida nodded. "I'm sorry."

"Thank you." he answered. "I'm sorry you never got to know her. She was a wonderful woman. We were married over sixty years."

"I've heard only good things about her," Ida said.

For some reason she couldn't quite understand, a slight feeling of jealousy rose in her.

That night, as the sun began to set, she heard his voice through the wall. He was talking to his dead wife again. The voice got louder, the sobs stronger. He was probably lighting the candle, reliving all the memories.

We all have memories, she said to herself, but sometimes we have to put them on the shelf and get on with our lives instead of wallowing in pity.

Well, let him live his last days the way he chose. She would be different. There was a dance around the pool area later that evening. She would go for the first time and enjoy watching the couples. Let Morris mourn day and night. He was none of her business.

She put her hands over her ears to drown out the sound of his voice as she went into the bedroom to get dressed.

"Life has to go on, Albert," she said to the photograph on the dresser. "Life has to go on."

MORRIS TOUCHED A MATCH TO THE YAHRTZEIT CANDLE and watched the flame waver. He stared into the glow, swallowed hard, then walked to the window of his apartment.

The setting sun threw a shadow across the buildings in the condominium complex. Balding, big-bellied men packed up their tennis racquets, wiped sweat from their wrinkled faces and started home. Probably to a waiting dinner and loving wife, Morris thought.

"Leah, I miss you so much," he whispered. "So many years we were together, side by side. Never one without the other. Maybe soon, we'll be together again in *ganedin*, in paradise."

Morris walked to the living room and took a photo album from the shelf. He lit a cigar and drew deeply. His fingers idled at every picture as he turned pages. Leah's face smiled to him from every one.

"It seems like only yesterday," he said to a picture of young Leah on their honeymoon.

She was his *barsherta*, his destined one. It was a marriage arranged by their parents, but he always said he was sure it was really made in heaven. He fell in love with her the first time he saw her.

Leah was eighteen years old, he was twenty. It was time for a *shidach*. Time to get married and start a family.

Morris' father made him a new suit for the meeting. His mother starched the collar of his good shirt, helped him trim his mustache and splashed cologne on his face before they went to the Little Hungarian Restaurant.

He could hardly eat his dinner that night. The goulash and kugel swam untouched in the gravy on his plate. Even the rich dessert couldn't compare to the beauty across from him. He watched her cheeks turn pink when she caught his glance, saw her lower her eyes in embarrassment.

Morris sighed now as he turned the pages of the album. Leah was sitting on a chair, her satin wedding gown spread all around her. Morris stood beside her in a cut-away tuxedo, his thick black hair plastered neatly with Vaseline, one hand resting on Leah's shoulder.

He frowned as he remembered the wedding night. He was all fingers as he fumbled with the buttons on her lace nightgown. She cried the first time they made love.

"It got better over the years, Leah, didn't it? We learned together, no?"

Morris closed the album and walked back to the yahrtzeit glass. The flame was stronger, licking against the sides of the glass. He felt heat radiating from it and imagined seeing Leah's face jumping at him from the fire.

"What do the young people today know from love like ours?" He asked himself. "All they know about is jumping from one to another, no commitment, no nothing. Even our own children and grandchildren. What do they know about such love? Sixty years we had together, Leah. Sixty beautiful years of building a successful business, raising a family. How can I go on without you now? There's nothing left for me. Nobody needs me. The children and grandchildren have their own lives. I'm nothing, nobody. My life is worthless."

Morris walked to the window. The sky had turned dark with a few stars scattered across it. A thin sliver of moon was barely visible. He threw his shoulders back and sighed. This was the kind of night Leah loved. He could picture her face and almost hear her voice. "Go, Morris, take your walk along the beach like you always did on a night like this. It's nice and pleasant. I'll be waiting for you. Go."

Morris took the elevator down to the lobby. He hardly looked at the other tenants as he hurried to the beach.

Sand trickled through his thongs as he walked toward the water's edge. Funny, he thought, how the air is always cooler on Miami Beach, the wind a little stronger.

Ripples of waves rolled toward the shore and splashed against his feet. He looked across the wide expanse of water, remembering the day he and his parents had come across this ocean and landed at Ellis Island. That had been the start of a new life. Maybe this same ocean could help him end his life.

Morris stared up at the stars. Leah seemed to be calling to him. Today was her yahrtzeit, the anniversary of her death. If he walked into the water and let the waves roll over him and fill his lungs, they would be together again.

He turned his head at the sound of music from the pool area. He saw men and women dancing together like he and Leah used to dance. Maybe Ida, the lady next door was there. She reminded him a little bit of Leah. A pretty lady with blue eyes and white hair piled on top of her head. She always smelled so nice. And her chicken soup and matzoh balls were so delicious, almost as good as Leah's.

Morris shook the sand from his feet and hurried back to the condo to get dressed. Life has to go on, he told himself. Life has to go on. ח

Giselle

"My name is Giselle Rabinowitz."

Red blotches formed on her pasty face at the muffled giggles in the classroom. The muscle in her right eye twitched as it always did when she was nervous.

"Thank you, Giselle. Welcome to our fifth grade class at McIntyre Elementary School. You may sit down now."

Giselle slid her scrawny body behind the desk, careful to avoid looking at any of her classmates. Her cheeks still burned and the muscle twitched harder. She picked at a chewed down nail, put her finger in her mouth and sucked the blood.

"Oh, God," she prayed, "Let this day end."

The sole of her shoe flip-flopped as she walked from school. The glue had come undone and the cardboard inside slid around.

"Hi, Giselle. I'm Annie. This is Ruthie. We're in your class. We sit two rows behind you."

She jumped at the sound of the voice. The muscle in her eye twitched again. She fought hard to control it, but it was impossible.

She had seen the two girls at school, envied the

ease with which they answered the teacher's questions, watched them from a secluded spot in the playground as they dominated every activity and seen the finger pointing and giggles aimed at her.

"Hi," she stammered. "Glad to meet you." She knew her face must be the color of the faded rose print on her dress.

"Where do you live? Where do you come from?" They moved closer to her on the narrow sidewalk, almost knocking her down.

"I used to live in South Philly. I just moved to Strawberry Mansion."

"We've lived in Strawberry Mansion all our lives. Well, nice to see you. We're on our way to the Park Movies to see *The Wizard of Oz*."

She heard their giggles and whispers as they walked away.

"Did you see the way her eye twitches when she talks? Wonder where she got that dumb name, Giselle?"

Giselle turned toward Fairmount Park. She didn't want to go home. She didn't care if it was Friday and the house would smell of *challah* and chicken soup and the *kiddush* cup would be waiting to be filled with sweet cherry wine. Tomorrow morning, when her father went to *shul* to pray, she would stay in her room praying for revenge.

She stepped on a pile of leaves. The crackling sound was good, as if Ruthie and Annie were being crunched under her feet.

Giselle walked up a winding path next to a small stream. She leaned down and cupped cool water in her hands and splashed it on her burning face.

Far below her, small boats sailed across the murky waters of the Schuylkill River. Across the Girard Avenue Bridge came the faint chimes of church bells.

Giselle sat down on the damp ground, leaned her head against the trunk of a maple tree and brushed large tear drops from her cheeks.

"We're going to see *The Wizard of Oz*," she mimicked the two girls. Well, it wouldn't have killed them to ask her if she wanted to go with them. How did they know she didn't have a dime anyway?

"Loony tune," she'd heard them say. "Wonder where she got that dumb name, Giselle?" Well, it wasn't always Giselle. Once it had been Gittel. Gittel Rabinowitz. She made up the name Giselle. Just like she made up so many other things. Let them spend their dime to see *The Wizard of Oz*. She would *be* the Wizard of Oz. She could be anyone she wanted to be.

Out here in the park, with only the trees and grass and rippling waters, she entered her own private world. Under a beautiful sky with clouds that looked like fluffy white marshmallows, next to chirping crickets and fluttering butterflies, she became Snow White, Rapunzel and Juliet.

"Romeo, oh, Romeo. Wherefore art thou, Romeo?"

Her voice echoed back to her through the quiet of the trees.

"Some day I'll show them all for making fun of me," she shouted down to the smelly river.

Banners reading STRAWBERRY MANSION FIFTY YEAR REUNION fluttered under the air conditioner vents. The hotel ballroom was filled to capacity. It wasn't every day that a famous movie star came to one of the reunions. Especially one who had once lived in Strawberry Mansion.

Jennifer Rogers stood behind the satin curtain, waiting for her introduction. She smiled at her reflection in the large mirror backstage, delighted at the way the years had treated her.

She tucked a strand of ash blond hair in her chignon. She had to be perfectly groomed for tonight's occasion. Everything must be exactly as she always rehearsed it.

Jennifer moved gracefully to the podium and cleared her throat. From the corner of her eye she recognized Ruthie and Annie seated at the head table. They were slightly overweight. Dark roots peeked through their bleached hair. Wrinkles criss-crossed their faces. The years apparently had not been as kind to them as they had been to her. She ran her hands over her slim hips and flat stomach, glad she never had babies to spoil her figure.

It hadn't been easy; the break from her family, stepping on people along the way, the lying and compromising to reach the top. But it was worth it. Tonight was the ultimate payback. She couldn't wait to see the envy on their faces.

Jennifer took a deep breath, about to speak. She looked again at Ruthie and Annie. Suddenly, she found herself back in Fairmount Park, the words "loony tune" echoing in her ears. Black ants scurried near her feet. The smell of the Schuylkill River reeked through the tall trees, choking her, gagging her. She felt red blotches pop up on her flawless skin.

It was impossible to stop the wild twitch in her right eye. ∎

The Good Old Days

"Look what I made on my computer, Grandma."

Joshua's face was pink from the cold air. Bits of snow fell from his ski suit and landed near my feet. I breathed in the sweet innocent smell of his body as he struggled out of his jacket. "Computers? They have computers in elementary school?"

He wrinkled his nose. "Come on, Grandma. Sure they have computers."

"Even in the second grade?"

"Sure. Even in kindergarten. What grade did they have them in when you went to school?"

I laughed. "When I went to school? There were no such things as computers in those days."

Joshua climbed onto my lap and cuddled against me, his wide brown eyes staring into my face. For a moment I tried to remember who he was, my son, my grandson or my great-grandson. They all had the same brown eyes, the small freckled nose.

His laugh reminded me that this was Joshua, my great-grandson. There was something about his laugh that was his alone.

"Come on, Grandma, stop joking. How could you

do your homework without a computer?"

"Well, Josh, in my day we learned the ABC's. We didn't need computers. Our brains were good enough."

He laughed again and leaned his head against me. I ran my fingers through his thick dark hair. His father and grandfather had thick dark hair once. Now his father's hair was thinning and his grandfather was completely bald.

"Would you like a slice of Sara Lee cake and a glass of milk, Joshua?" I thought for a minute about how my grandmother always had a freshly baked treat for me when I visited her. I can still smell the delicious cinnamon buns warm and gooey from her oven. Sometimes I was tempted to bake like she did, but why compete with Sara Lee?

"No, thanks. Mommy got me a yogurt on the way home from school.

My leg started to turn numb from the bony tush bearing down on it, but I hated to push him off. My moments with him were all too few and the years have a way of racing along.

His little fingers played along the wrinkles on my face. I knew the question before he asked it. "Grandma, why does your face have so many lines?"

"Because I'm an old lady, Josh, and when people get old, lots of things change." I tried to smile, but for some reason, my lips turned into a frown as I waited for the next question.

"Are you gonna die soon? I saw a show on TV and the lady was old and she got sick and died."

I hugged him tighter. The numbness in my leg had traveled down to my calf. I shifted his weight a little and tried to change the subject.

"I don't want you to die. I would miss you."

"Well, I'm not planning to die soon, so don't you worry."

I tried to remember if death was ever discussed when I was a child or when my children were young.

What isn't discussed now, I wondered. This is a modern world. A world of computers and now internets. Instead of innocence, children know about sex and violence and death before they know how to tie their shoelaces. Instead of Howdy Doody, they see MTV and condom commercials. Oh, for the good old days!

The numbness reached my ankles. Soon, my toes would be asleep. I eased Joshua off my lap just as his mother tooted the horn.

I watched from my window as they drove away. The trees on the condo lawn were bare, the sky a dismal gray. The glow had disappeared from the horizon.

I thought again about the good old days when

movies cost a dime, candy cost a penny and a great big cone of ice cream covered with jimmies was three cents. Then I remembered how difficult it was to save up enough money for those luxuries during the depression. I saw my mother scrubbing clothes on a washboard in a dark cellar and hanging them on the line in our small back yard. I heard the bed sheets flapping in the wind and smelled the garbage and animal droppings from the alley.

My stomach growled thinking about the times it lacked food in those "good old days." Were they really so good?

Time was growing shorter. I went to my room and put fresh make-up on, trying to mask some of the wrinkles.

There would be just enough time to throw some clothes in the washer and dryer, thaw out a hamburger patty for dinner, then go to the rec room for my yoga class and a game of canasta. Later tonight, there's a dance at the clubhouse.

The leaves on the tree might be dead and buried, but a lot of life still clings to the roots.

The Partners

Amplified music blasted through the thick wooden doors of the reception hall. Meyer covered his ears with his hands and grimaced.

"I couldn't stay in there another minute. Did you ever hear such garbage? This is music? Give me the good old days when music was really music."

Joseph nodded. "Everything is different nowadays. Everything is competition. The *Bar Mitzvahs* are bigger and more expensive and everybody has to have a theme. Famous movies themes, football heroes themes, space themes. Everything has to be better and more expensive than the last one."

Meyer clasped his friend's shoulder. "You remember, Joseph, in our day what a *Bar Mitzvah* was like? I was lucky if my father could afford a bottle of *shnopps* to take to *shul* for the *kiddush*. My mother cooked and baked all week for the celebration. The house smelled from her gefilte fish and brisket and chopped herring. Who needed a caterer? Who knew from such things?"

Joseph smiled. "Did you see the suit on Scott this morning? A silk suit, made to order, the *pisher* needed? And the *tallis* from Israel. Hah! I remember my first pair of long pants for my *Bar Mitzvah* and the woolen *tallis* my father wrapped around my shoulders. But today, everything is competition. Whatever one boy has, the next one must have more. Better he should have practiced his *Haftorah* more. I counted three mistakes he made."

"Only three? I counted at least five." Meyer tugged at the bow tie around his neck. "These black tie affairs make me sick. Everything feels tighter after eating all the hors d'ouvres. By the time they serve the dinner, you feel like a stuffed pig. Come, let's take a little walk outside to make room for the desserts they'll soon set up in the hall."

The streets were quiet and dark. They circled the block, counting the cars lined up along the curb, the Lincolns and Cadillacs and Jaguars.

"That's another thing," Joseph said. "Everybody has a car now. Whoever saw so many cars in our day? You walked where you had to go. Who had money for a car?"

Meyer laughed. "Money? We hardly knew what the word meant until we opened the factory. I thought I was rich when I counted up a hundred and fifty dollars from my *Bar Mitzvah* along with the five or six fountain pens. Today, you're a piker if you don't make out a nice check for a present. I was ready to give Scott three hundred dollars, then I found out that Lou gave my grandson five hundred for his *Bar Mitzvah*, so I knew I had to give the same. God forbid, Lou should have something to say. You know how he always had to top us even when we were all partners.

Meyer was silent for a moment. He put his hand in his trouser pocket and fingered the card and check he had for the boy. "Let's go back to the hall. I have to use the men's room before they bring out the dessert."

He ducked quickly into one of the stalls and stared at the three hundred dollar check he had written, ripped it into tiny pieces and watched it swirl down the toilet, grateful that he always carried a blank check and a pen in case of emergencies. With a deep sigh, he wrote Scott's name on the new check for five hundred and fifty dollars."

Joseph listened to the sounds from Meyer's stall, the crisp paper being torn, the hurried flush of the toilet, the scratching of a pen.

He closed the door of a stall at the other end of the room and chuckled as he wrote a new check in the amount of six hundred dollars.

Six Months

"Sadie, is that you? Is this the Sadie Cohen I took care of so many years ago? You look positively gorgeous. You haven't aged a day. What is your secret?"

Sadie stared at the woman beside her, the woman who had helped her through the most trying period of her life. There was no question that this was her nurse, Miss Wilson.

Her eyes grew wet as she pulled the woman to her, all the old emotions rose in her as she remembered that day so long ago, a week after her surgery.

Dr. Anderson's voice had carried through the open door. His distinctive accent and clipped tones and hurried speech were as much his trade mark as the sharp click of his heels as he rushed from one patient to another.

"Ovarian cancer. We're starting radiation therapy tomorrow, but it won't help. I give her six months."

Six months! She sat upright in bed. He was talking about her in such a matter-of-fact manner. It didn't mean a thing to him that she was only twenty-four, that her whole life was ahead of her.

It took a long time for Miss Wilson to calm her down. She stroked her face. "Nobody should ever make statements like that. He's not God, even if he thinks he is.

There's a power much higher than any doctor. The only thing Dr. Anderson knows for sure is how many rounds of golf he can play in a week."

Sadie tried to remember Nurse Wilson's words each day as she lay under the X-ray machine. "He's not God," she kept telling herself, but she was hardly convinced.

She watched her children at play. Her son, the preemie who looked like a plucked chicken at birth, now a precocious three year old with curly blond hair and a happy smile. Her daughter, barely a year old, a happy, gurgling baby with blue eyes, tiny nose and dimpled cheeks. She wondered if they would remember her when she was gone.

Four months passed. Winter turned to spring. Birds sang and flowers poked their heads up from the cold ground. "I'll never see the changing seasons again." she cried to her husband, but there was no consoling her.

Five months went by. Her body weakened from the massive radiation. Soon it would be over. Dr. Anderson's death sentence approached.

It was time to get ready. How? Did she set a platter of cookies next to the fireplace for the Angel of Death like people set goodies for Santa Claus?

She went to the synagogue where she had walked down the aisle as a young bride five years earlier.

Her body shook as she entered the chapel. The room was quiet, peaceful. The paneled walls smelled of pine. She looked at the Ten Commandments on the wall, the *Ner Tamid* shining above the Ark and she prayed for a message from God.

All she heard was the sound of Miss Wilson's voice as she comforted her that day. "He's not God," she had said, "even if he thinks he is. The only thing he knows for certain is how many rounds of golf he can play in a week."

That was forty-five years ago. She linked her arm through Miss Wilson's and walked toward the buffet table, happy to be alive and part of this convention of cancer survivors.

Miss Wilson squeezed Sadie's hand. "You don't know how I've worried about you. I moved out of town shortly after your surgery, but I never forgot you. Now, you have given me hope. I'm in my fourth year of recovery from breast cancer." She looked around the room. "By the way, is Dr. Anderson here? I imagine he must be thrilled to know how wrong he was."

"Didn't you know?" Sadie answered. "Dr. Anderson was killed forty-five years ago. He was struck by lightning on the golf course exactly six months after my operation."

Rock Candy

A hot summer sun shone down on the narrow South Philadelphia street, reflecting off crumbling brick walls and broken concrete steps. Today, the houses were to be torn down to make way for a high-rise apartment complex.

Blanche had come to say "goodbye."

She was barely aware of the small, frail woman standing near her until she heard her voice.

"Did you used to live here?" There was something vaguely familiar about the accent. She moved closer to Blanche's side. Although her face was deeply lined, her blue eyes looked clear and ageless.

Blanche stared at the woman before she answered. "Yes. I lived here a long time ago when I was just a little girl. Soon it will be gone like everything else in life. Nothing lasts forever.

The woman's voice was soft. "Memories last forever."

Blanche nodded. "You're right. Memories do last forever." She closed her eyes for a moment and the years drifted back. She was a child of six, standing at the door to one of these houses, nervously clutching her sister's arm. Her grandmother reached out and drew her inside.

She heard happy childish laughter once more as

she played hopscotch on the sidewalk and roller skated down the streets across bumpy cobblestones.

Corner stores came alive. Fat salamis on long cords hung from the ceiling in the delicatessen. There were pickles and tomatoes. Herrings swam again in big wooden barrels filled with brine.

She tasted the creamy ice cream from the candy store. It melted under the hot sun and trickled down her hand as she skipped home to her grandmother. In her other hand, she held a bag of rock candy. Her grandmother put one crystal in her mouth and stuffed the rest in her pocket for later. She winked to Blanche as if to say "thank you."

In the autumn, when the leaves turned red and golden orange, they walked home from *shul* just as the lamplighter came down the street with his ladder tucked beneath his arm. He propped the wooden ladder against the pole outside their house and touched the wick with his taper. Like magic, the street came alive with the flickering light.

"Hey, lady, you'd better get going. We're gonna be blasting soon."

The gruff voice from the demolition truck brought her back to the present. The wrecking crew stood in the middle of the street, where trolley tracks once lay and the milkman's horse and wagon passed so long ago.

Blanche reached out to steer the old woman away

from danger. Her hand touched an empty space. At the corner of the street, where there used to be a *shul*, she saw the small figure retreating. A glow surrounded her.

The old woman turned and stared, then placed something in her mouth. Slowly, she stuffed a small paper bag securely in her pocket, winked, and shuffled out of sight.

A bright crystal glistened near Blanche's feet. It shone like a clear-cut diamond. She picked the rock candy up and held it in her hand. With one last look at her old house, she walked away.

The Dilemma

To go or not to go, that was the question. To discuss it with my husband was another big decision. The problem was far from simple.

You see, I lead a double life. Most of the time, I'm a rather quiet, refined, normal human being. Some even describe me as mild mannered. But when my Miami Dolphins play, another personality emerges, transforming me into a raving maniac. This was my problem.

The Dolphins were to play the Green Bay Packers at 1PM at Joe Robbie Stadium. At my Temple, the scene was being set for Rosh Hashana services to begin at 7PM.

Rosh Hashana, the start of the New Year is the holiest time in Jewish life. The Rabbi leads us in prayer as we start our ten days of repentance, culminating on Yom Kippur, the Day of Atonement, a time of deepest introspection.

How would the Rabbi react if, for some reason the game went into overtime, or I got held up in traffic and came late to the Temple? Would it upset or humiliate him? After all, the Rabbi's wife shouldn't ever be late.

I watched as he took his white clerical robe, prayer shawl and skullcap from the closet and placed it on the bed. "How come you're not getting ready?" he asked.

I tried to mask my frustration. "It's only eleven

o'clock. Services don't start until seven."

"I'm not talking about services, I mean the football game."

"You mean you won't mind if I go to the game before Rosh Hashana?" My heart raced as I reached for my Dolphin shirt, the lucky one sure to guarantee a win. The maniac rose to the surface.

"Of course I won't mind. You'll be back in plenty of time. Go and enjoy yourself."

The rest of his words almost escaped me because I was out of the door and halfway to the stadium while he was still speaking.

It was a perfect day for football. The sky looked clear and a slight breeze cooled the air.

Bright colored uniforms dotted the field. The Dolphins in aqua and orange warmed up on one side and the Packers in green and gold practiced hand offs and passes at the other.

I settled back in my seat, the pre-game jitters slowly fading as I thought about how we were favored to win by at least two touchdowns. I knew the odds makers were never wrong. Besides, I had on my lucky shirt.

Then my husband's parting words came back to me. "Shirl, you know I always root for the Dolphins, but I have a problem today. A former Bar Mitzvah student is a rookie for the Packers. He's #73. I can't root against him. I'm sure you understand."

Understand? Never. I could only hope that G-d would pay more attention to a Rabbi's prayers for his congregants than a silly football game.

Through my binoculars, I searched the field for the little boy whose picture hung on the office wall. The little Bar Mitzvah boy looking at his Rabbi with such love and affection. The little boy who had suddenly become a menace.

There he was, #73. My, how he had grown in ten years. Biceps bulged from his uniform, massive shoulders jutted from a neck the size of a tree trunk. He held his helmet and his blond hair shone under the Miami sun. He looked nothing like the skinny little boy on the photograph.

Please, succeed in your profession. Make it to the Pro Bowl, even the Hall of Fame, but don't do too well today. I may not have influence with the football commissioner, but I might be able to have your Bar Mitzvah rescinded. These thoughts ran around and around in my head.

1PM. Miami won the toss. First down. Marino took the snap, faded back and threw the ball to Mark Duper. Duper sailed into the end zone untouched.

I relaxed in my seat. The game was in the bag. Maybe I would be able to leave before the end of the fourth quarter, beat the traffic and get home early. I would try hard not to gloat about how we beat the Packers. Gloating would not be proper on such a solemn day.

2:30PM. The score was 16 to 0. When it reached 35 to 0, I would definitely leave. Maybe there would be time for a nap before dressing for Temple.

2:50PM. Green Bay received the ball in the second half. Within two minutes, they moved down the field and scored a touchdown. The quarterback had great protection, our defense couldn't get near him, thanks to the wonderful job the rookie, #73, was doing.

I stiffened in my seat. My ice cream popsicle melted down my hand, trailed down my lucky shirt and landed on my aqua pants, leaving a large chocolate stain.

This wasn't supposed to happen. The Dolphins were supposed to win. Darn that #73! The thought of murder crossed my mind, but only briefly. Today was a day to be pure of thought.

3:45PM. By the fourth quarter, I grew less tense. The score was now 23 to 10 in favor of the Dolphins. Only a few minutes remained on the clock. The Packers were not a come-back team. I smiled with confidence.

My mind skipped ahead, picturing myself arriving at the Temple. I heard the beautiful choir, felt the reverence of the holiday, the warmth of the congregants. Slowly, my other personality rose. Hostility faded away. Once more, I became the gentle *Rebbitzin*, the Rabbi's wife, and no one would ever guess the madness that overtook me earlier.

A collective moan from the crowd pulled me back to the stadium. Touchdown! The Packers scored. It was probably my fault. My momentary distraction had done it. It was now 23 to 17 with only minutes left to play.

4:30PM. The Dolphins had the ball. All Marino had to do was run out the clock.

Fumble!

The Packers took over and moved down to our five yard line.

4:50PM. Six seconds left. Almost a lifetime. There was no stopping them. Rookie #73 gave the quarterback all the time he needed.

The entire crowd rose to its feet, shouting, stomping, trying to stop the inevitable. Everyone but me. I kept my eyes focused on the spreading stain on my pants, hardly daring to breathe. I heard another loud groan. Green Bay scored a touchdown. With the conversion point, they would win.

A loud cheer went up in the crowd. A yellow flag dropped to the ground. A penalty! One of the Packers had jumped offside!

The official's voice was loud and clear over the speaker. "Offside, offense. #73. Five yard penalty."

No touchdown! The Dolphins won the game, 23

to 17.

5:35PM. The game was so close, all I could think of was praying for the Dolphins to win. It hadn't dawned on me that everyone else would feel that way and would stay until the very end. Traffic was at a standstill and I had to get home and prepare for Temple!

6:20PM. I didn't think I would ever get home. I ran into the house, in and out of the shower, slipped into my clothes and dashed to the Temple.

7PM. I arrived at the Temple in my new holiday outfit. The congregants nodded approvingly. "Such a refined lady," I heard someone whisper.

All around me, I felt the sanctity of the holiday spirit as the Cantor and the choir chanted the beautiful liturgy.

I looked at my husband on the pulpit and wondered if he was upset at the Packers loss or if he really hoped, for my sake, the Dolphins would win.

Before he started his sermon, he smiled and raised his hand in a "V" sign.

I leaned back in my seat. The maniac disappeared...until the next game.

Minnie

A strong force held me at the door, the envelope in my hand. It would have been so easy to just return it to the mailman, but I felt compelled to deliver it myself and not pay attention to the warning that rumbled in my head.

In spite of the summer heat, a cold chill traveled through me. I ran my tongue across my lips. They felt dry, chapped. My heartbeat sounded louder than my knock at the door.

It was unusual for me to go out of my way for a stranger. I was too timid, to face new situations. But I no longer had free will. A power too strong to resist took possession of me the moment I saw the letter.

The handwriting, like the stamps, was from another country, but I felt as if I had seen it before.

An old woman opened the door. She tried to smile, but the obvious effects of a stroke pulled the right side of her mouth down. I held the envelope out to her. "This was sent to my house by mistake."

Tiny eyes squinted up at me then moved to the letter in my hand. I offered it to her and she held it close, examining the address. "Thank you. It's a letter from my cousin in Israel. You were very kind to bring it to me.

Come in. Come in for a few minutes. It's so hot outside. Maybe you would like a cold drink."

"Don't go," a voice inside me warned. "Your life will never be the same."

"My name is Minnie," the old woman said.

I nodded. I knew her name from the envelope, but something told me I would have known it anyway.

The little house looked like an antique shop. Chantilly figurines and music boxes filled every space. A sour, musty smell crept through the pungent odor of Pine Sol on formal, high-backed Victorian chairs and ornate velvet sofas covered with doilies.

Minnie opened the blinds and sun peeked through the lace curtains on the windows, throwing rays of light across cut-glass vases, crystal bowls and dozens of knick-knacks scattered on mahogany tables.

I didn't belong there. I was generations removed from this old woman; so different from me in every respect. Her face was covered with criss-cross lines. Sagging jowls hung over the high collar of her print blouse. Around her waist she wore a muted print apron edged in colorful ric-rac. Orthopedic shoes supported bulging ankles.

Minnie poured a glass of soda with shaking hands. "What's your name?" she asked.

"Nancy."

"Nancy. That's a nice name. You seem very kind. Why don't you sit down and cool off for a few minutes? August is so hot in Miami. Or maybe you have more important things to do?"

"No, not really. I'm in my last year at the University and this is summer vacation." I was happy to sit down. Standing next to her, my five foot frame felt gigantic. The humped back had shriveled her to almost dwarf-like proportions, causing her head to jut forward on her chest.

As I sipped my soda, my eyes kept wandering to the photographs in her hall; photographs from another era, another world. The same indescribable feeling I had experienced at the door overcame me again, as if I had stumbled into a web that would hold me captive for the rest of my life.

The people came alive, staring back with an intensity that made me shiver. Men in dark, somber suits, and women wearing prim, long sleeved dresses were unsmiling, but a quiet dignity surrounded them like the shawls draped on their heads. I could almost hear them speak to me, but the language was unfamiliar.

Minnie followed my look. "The tall man was my father," she said. "He was a famous doctor in Russia, right on the border of the Ukraine." She wiped her hands on her apron. "Come, take a closer look and I'll tell you what a wonderful doctor he was and how handsome he was."

Shadows fell across my bed that night. I tossed back and forth, revisiting the faces on Minnie's wall. Dark eyes stalked me, accused me of something I could never have been guilty of doing. I was born long after these people had died.

There had to be a logical explanation. A book, movie or TV show must have made a lasting impression on me. Maybe I once knew people who looked like them.

I shivered as I thought of my own father; his icy blue stare, his fists that lashed out when he was in one of his drunken rages.

Careful not to disturb Peter and risk his anger, I slid out of bed. I held my breath as he stirred, then turned on his side.

The night was clear. A full, pale moon shone in the sky. A few stars scattered their light across the dark. I stood at the window and watched the curtains sway in the breeze. I still felt that strange attraction toward Minnie and her people. They were so different from anyone with whom I had come in contact. Perhaps that's why their images kept me awake.

I returned to the old woman's home several times, a strong bond drawing me to this funny looking little lady whose broken English I could barely understand.

Coffee always brewed in her kitchen, freshly baked cake sat on the table. She awaited my visits with a hunger that matched my own. She told me much of her early life in Russia, yet she revealed nothing.

"Tell me about your father. What was he like when you were growing up?"

The answer was always the same. "He was a famous doctor. And he was handsome...so handsome. I loved him very much."

"And your mother?"

She turned her head away, but not in time to hide the tears. "She died when I was a little girl."

Wherever I went, the pictures on the wall followed me. At night they invaded my sleep. My thoughts dwelled on them day and night.

"What's the problem?" Peter stood behind me, fully awake now, his arms around my waist. "What the hell's been bothering you lately? You going nuts? You're always a million miles away."

"Nothing's wrong, Peter," I lied. "I'm fine. It must be the heat. Go back to bed."

His arms tightened, pressing harder, squeezing against my ribs. "You'd better not be keeping anything from me," he said.

As the first rays of dawn threw colors across the

sky, I crept into bed and fell into a deep sleep.

Heavy footsteps trudged through snow covered lanes. Thousands of people, shouting, jeering, laughing, ran through the woods. Rifle shots rang out over and over. Terrified voices shouted, "Help us! Help us!"

Peter shook me, slapped my face. "Wake up, Nancy! You must have been dreaming. You were sobbing so damn loud you could wake the dead. And you were rambling in some strange language. When did you learn something like that? Look at yourself. Your whole body is soaking wet. What in the hell is going on? "

I rubbed my hand across the welts on my face. "I'm sorry. I was having a nightmare. I'm OK now. Please, go to the office before you're late. I'll get up in a few minutes and take a shower."

He kissed me where his hand had struck. "I didn't mean to slap you, but you're driving me nuts. You'd better shape up by the time I get home."

The warm water felt good on my clammy body. I twisted and turned, letting the spray cover me from head to toe.

"Ninotchka!"

I cocked my head and listened.

"Ninotchka!"

The voices were loud and clear, the language foreign, but I understood it. I covered my ears to try to drown out the sounds, but they grew louder and louder.

Steam from the shower evaporated and turned to ice. I was freezing. Wind swirled around me. Frantically, I tried to turn the shower off, but the knobs were frozen in place. Sobbing, I pounded on the tile walls as the shouts continued.

"Ninotchka, help us! Help us!"

I jumped from the shower, slipping on the floor. My hand grasped the towel rack and broke my fall. I stumbled back to bed, dripping wet, and pulled the covers over my head. But nothing could block the voices that roared all around me.

"Nancy, come in, come in." Minnie grinned and wiped the corner of her twisted mouth with the back of her hand. "I was hoping you would come today. I baked some fresh buns. Come, dear, I'll pour you a nice cup of coffee."

I gulped the coffee down and nibbled a cinnamon bun. It was the first bit of food I had eaten all day.

"What's the matter you didn't come for a few days? I missed your visits. It's so nice to see such a pretty face. You remind me of someone I knew a long time ago in Russia." She had a faraway look each time she mentioned her past.

I picked at the raisins in the bun, my head turned toward the portraits on the wall. They were alive, reaching out, pleading, begging me for something. But what? They had become my obsession.

"I guess you're anxious to get back to school after the summer. Education is so important. When I was a little girl, my father always said to me, "Malke, that's my Hebrew name, Malke, what you put into your brain, nobody can ever take away from you. He was a smart man, my father. Did I tell you he was a famous doctor? Nancy, you're not even listening to me. I could be talking to the walls. You're so busy looking at the pictures, you don't even know I'm here." She walked to the stove and poured another cup of coffee.

"Who was Ninotchka?" I asked.

The cup dropped from her hands, crashed to the tile floor, and shattered into pieces. The brown liquid splashed across her apron and down the swollen legs. She sat hard on the kitchen chair clasping her chest and gasping for air.

"My God," I shouted. "What did I say? Are you all right?"

"It's all right. I have a little angina. I'll be okay in a minute." She slipped a pill under her tongue. "The stockings are thick so I'm not burned."

I wiped the coffee from the floor and carefully

picked up the broken glass, my eyes glued to hers.

"What do you know about Ninotchka? Where did you hear that name? Did I ever mention her to you?"

"No, never. The name came to me from the air. I heard voices calling, "Ninotchka, Ninotchka, help us." It happens over and over, driving me crazy. They speak in a foreign language, but I understand every word. Who was she? How did these thoughts get through to me?"

Minnie's face looked gray and I was afraid she would have another attack. Her hands shook as she searched for a tissue in her apron pocket. More saliva oozed from her mouth.

"Since you came here that day, I took to you like a long lost relative. But it's no good. It's like a dybbuk has been let loose. I remember things I thought were out of my memory forever. Oh, God, if only my Meyer were still alive to help me understand. A dybbuk, that's what it is. A dybbuk!" She fanned herself with her tissue.

"A dybbuk? What's a dybbuk?" I asked.

"A dybbuk is a devil. A devil has come into my soul, making me remember things I want to forget. Bad things instead of happy memories. Who needs to remember bad things?"

I put my arms around her and felt her stiffen. "Do you think I'm responsible for this dybbuk? Do you want me to leave?"

"No. Don't go. I don't know what's happening, but I wait for your visits. You're like a special granddaughter. I have nobody since my Meyer died, his soul should rest in peace. The family is all dead. We lost everybody in the war. Everybody except my cousin in Israel. All the neighbors here keep to themselves and besides, I like you because you're a nice girl. You don't make fun of an old lady and her silly talk. About Ninotchka, we'll talk some day. But not today. Come, finish your coffee and I'll tell you some more happy stories about my father. Did I tell you how handsome he was? Even more handsome than on the picture. You know, he was a famous doctor in Russia."

THE BRIDGE WAS UP ON MACARTHUR CAUSEWAY. I watched a boat pass beneath it, aqua water rippling in its wake. The view from the bridge was beautiful. I stared across to Miami Beach where tall, majestic hotels stood outlined against the horizon.

Miami Beach was my haven when pressure mounted. Sometimes, after a fight with Peter, the serenity of the ocean and sand comforted me.

The beach was crowded. I walked to the edge of the water, my feet digging into the wet sand, toes scraping small pieces of sea shells. The sun felt hot on my shoulders. I scooped up a handful of water and dribbled it on my body. Small waves broke on the shore, splattering against me. I walked farther into the ocean and floated, closing my eyes against the rays of the sun until the tension eased.

I kept thinking about a land across the ocean, on the other side of the continent. It was so far removed from anything in my life, but it continued to haunt me.

I was born in Tennessee to parents who constantly drank and fought and resented my presence. I grew up with racial and ethnic epithets ringing in my ears. My father hated anyone who wasn't white and Baptist. When he was drunk, my body ached from his punches. I could imagine what he would say or do if he knew of my involvement with a Jew.

Peter wasn't much different. I stayed with him out of fear and the convenience of the house his parents bought for him. His moods were unpredictable and more than once they led to abuse that always followed with an apology and love making. I was relieved when he left the University and got a full time job in an insurance office. Knowing how strongly he, too, felt about Jews, I was determined to keep my visits with Minnie a secret from him

"Nancy, I was beginning to worry about you. You weren't here for such a long time. I thought maybe you ran away some place. Come in, come in. Don't stand there. Even the coffee pot was missing you."

Minnie wore the same mismatched outfit she wore when I first saw her; a green print blouse that clashed with the reds and blues in her plaid skirt. A tissue peeked out of the apron around her bulging waist.

Her hair looked a little grayer, her face a little more wrinkled, but the familiar smile tried to form around her lips.

"So, what kept you so busy you couldn't find time for an old lady? My coffee, maybe, you didn't like anymore?"

"No, Minnie. I just couldn't get away." I couldn't tell her what an effort it had been not to come here, how hard I was trying to free my mind of many conflicting thoughts. "How have you been feeling?" I asked.

"For an old lady, I can't complain. Besides, what good would it do? There's nobody but you to pay attention anyway."

The photographs pulled at me again. I saw the little huts those people lived in, the thick woods surrounding them. I heard their voices, felt their pain. I shivered from the cold, snowy air. I was a part of them, barely aware of Minnie standing beside me, tugging at my sleeve.

I pointed to the picture of her mother, a beautiful woman with dark hair pulled back in a bun. Her brown eyes stared at me. "Why did they kill her?" I asked. "Why did they do it?"

Minnie clutched her chest. "How did you know

this? I never told you. What is happening? Who are you? Who sent you here?"

I grabbed her to keep her from falling. Her face was the color of lead. I helped her to a chair and watched her put the pill under her tongue.

"It frightens me, too. I don't know how I know some things. It's just there. Ever since I came here that day with your letter. There's something that links me with you and your past. Maybe it would be better if I left and never came back. This doesn't seem to be doing either one of us much good."

She waved her hands. "No. I look for your visits. Who else do I have? I'm all alone in the world." She blew her nose into her tissue. Color returned to her face. "Besides, I feel the pull, too. There's something between us that only God could understand. Please don't leave me. Soon the summer will be over and you'll be back in school and I'll be alone again."

Minnie took my hand. Her eyes were wet. "I never talk about her because it hurts so much. It happened when I was a little girl."

"The Cossaks. The damn, lousy Cossaks," I said.

"Yes, the Cossaks. I tried to put it out of my mind. Some things it's better not to remember. But since you started to come here, everything is coming back to me like it was yesterday." She grabbed her chest again, and for a moment, I was afraid she was going to pass out.

I stroked her hair. "Don't talk about it if it's too painful."

She stared straight ahead, shook her head and waved me off.

"I was only six years old. My mother was baking a cake. My father was in Medical School. The cake was for him; a cake for Shabbos. I remember how she used to let me lick the bowl. I still taste the sweet batter like it was yesterday. Then it happened. We heard the horses outside. I saw the look on my mother's face. She knew. She tried to hide me, but it was too late. They were there, inside our house. They smashed everything in sight, laughing and shouting while they did their dirty work."

Her face paled as she relived the event. Her breathing was rapid and again I was afraid, but there was no stopping the flow of words.

"They tied me to a chair. They forced me to watch while they tore off her clothes and took turns beating and raping her. There were four of them. I screamed and screamed until I couldn't scream anymore. They smacked me a few times and blood ran from my mouth and nose. My mother begged them not to hurt me, but they beat her harder. Her blood was all over the floor. After awhile, she was still and I knew she was dead. Maybe they didn't expect to kill her, I don't know, but all of a sudden they left. For years, I tried to forget how she looked there on the floor, her eyes staring up at the ceiling."

Minnie put her head on the table and sobbed.

Her mother's screams echoed in my ears. I was there. I could have told the story right along with her. I saw the clouds of dust kicked up by the retreating horses, heard the drunken laughter of the soldiers, smelled the blood and semen and death. I saw her mother's body lying lifeless on the floor, broken and twisted.

I was there, watching through a window, too terrified to run for help, frozen in place. Maybe if I had done something, her mother wouldn't have died.

"I'm sorry, I'm sorry," I mumbled. "I always seem to bring back terrible memories. Maybe it really would be better if I went away and didn't come back."

She looked up at me and a strong feeling bound us together. She grasped my hand and squeezed it. "No. Please don't stay away. Maybe it's better for me to talk like this. Maybe it's good for my soul. Maybe God wants me to remember everything before I join my Meyer. Don't ask me why, but from the first day you came here, I felt like I knew you all my life."

For a moment, we were silent. I stroked her hair and kissed her wrinkled face. "I feel it, too," I answered.

"Come, drink your coffee and eat your cake. We'll talk about better times. You know, my father went on to become a doctor. A famous doctor. Even the gentiles came to him. Everybody loved him. Did I tell you how handsome he was?"

That night, I stood at my window and tried to count the stars, but my mind kept wandering away.

It's so different in Miami, I thought. Nothing like the stark, cold days and nights in Russia, the endless winters.

But how could I know what it was like over there? I had never been out of the United States in my entire life.

At least not in *this* lifetime.

THE LIBRARY WAS FAIRLY QUIET during the month of August. Soon, students would come back to school and vacationers return home.

Stacks of books sat on the table in front of me. I thumbed through them until I found the ones I wanted.

Reincarnation. I had never thought about it. Now it was consuming me.

I tried to talk to Peter about it the night before, but he laughed at me. "Cut the crap," he said. "As far as I'm concerned, when you're dead, you're dead."

"How about this book by Dr. Brian Weiss? He

discovered lots of proof of former lives. Why don't you read it, then maybe you won't think it's a bunch of garbage."

He pushed my hand away. "Weiss? Another smart-ass Jew trying to make a buck off jerks like you. I'm telling you, when you're dead, you're dead."

I lay sleepless that night with the sounds of screams echoing in my ears. I saw open pits and thousands of lifeless bodies. The stench of death was everywhere.

Now I was searching for answers. Who was I in another life? What linkage did I have with Minnie and her people?

Reincarnation. It was the only explanation.

I ran my hands through my hair while leafing through the pages.

Reincarnation, Karma. It all made sense. It probably explained my reason for staying with Peter, accepting his frequent abuses, the ready fists when he was drunk or displeased with something I said or did, or didn't say or do. I had to be punished for sins in a former life.

Reincarnation; the Transmigration of the Soul. In ancient Greece, I read, the belief was that the soul was reborn after a period of retribution in Hades and passed from one body to another until it was purified. Then it reached Nirvana.

I put one of the books back on the shelf and stretched my legs. It was past lunch time and my stomach growled, but I couldn't leave the library.

I looked at the other students and wondered what their past lives had been. I turned back to the books.

What a person does determines what he will experience in his next life, I read. If you live a good life, you will be reborn as a human, rich or poor, beautiful or ugly. If you live like an animal, you will return as an animal.

Scenes of Russia and the Ukraine flashed before me. I felt sure many of the people there would return as animals.

I took another book from the shelf; a book on Judaism, wondering what the Judaic belief was. I turned the pages until I found a section on Cabalism, the Jewish Mystical sect.

Reincarnation was referred to as Gilgul, the belief that those who committed extreme sins are given the opportunity to come back to make amends. Cabalists believe that people are reincarnated in circumstances similar to their previous lives. Karma is the justice meted out to every individual in the form of reward or punishment. Every good or bad action will eventually be rewarded or punished.

I slammed the book shut. This was my answer, the reason for everything; my parents, Peter and now my chance meeting with Minnie and the thrust back to a former incarnation. Where would it lead me? What did I have to do to atone for my sins?

The sun beat down on me as I left the library and drove to Miami Beach. What a different world I lived in now compared to the frost and snow in Russia, the thick forests and muddy rivers.

On the Causeway, fathers and sons stood fishing, sailboats bobbed on the foamy waters. The car next to me vibrated to loud rock and roll music.

My favorite view appeared, the beautiful skyline of Miami Beach. Soon, I would float in the ocean and put all these confusing thoughts from my mind. I had to forget the past and stay away from Minnie before I went crazy.

Then I remembered reading a quote from George Santayana, "Those who don't learn from the past are doomed to repeat it."

This was my Karma. I would be linked with Minnie forever.

White seagulls flapped their wings, skimmed the waves, then swooped down on the beach. Their loud screeches blended with the sound of the bathers.

Far out in the ocean, a large ship moved slowly

across the waters. I stood at the edge, staring across the sea, deep in thought.

Peter was getting impatient with me. This morning was the worst scene.

"I don't know what the hell is eating you. You're like someone obsessed. And all your crazy talk about living before, and not being able to sleep, and the crazy language you come out with!" His face was red as he tugged at the zipper on his briefcase. "I'll tell you one thing, either you stop this crap or I'm throwing you out. This is my house, don't forget. Christ, I don't remember the last time we made love. You're looking for trouble, Nancy, I'm warning you."

"Please, Peter, bear with me. I'm going through a trying time." He pushed my hand away and threw me against the wall. His face looked like my father's face when he was angry.

Now, a small child pulled at my leg, breaking me away from that morning's fight. Large, dark eyes looked at me. The child's braids were shiny black with ribbons tied at their ends.

"Could you get my pail for me, please?" she said.

I was back in Russia. My body turned cold. "Raizel? Raizel? Where is Lilya? You have to get away before they come." I grabbed the tiny hand and started to run.

"Let go of her before I call a cop!" A short, stocky woman pulled the frightened child away. "Are you crazy?" she demanded. "Come, Suzanna, don't be frightened. Mommy will take care of you. What did I tell you about talking to strangers?"

Quickly, I left the beach and got to my car. I leaned my forehead against the steering wheel and waited for the banging in my head to stop before I put the key in the ignition.

Again, something had pushed me back to another life. Raizel and Lilya had needed me but I failed them. I couldn't remember where or when.

One thing I was sure of, this was the Karma meted out for me. There were sins I had to atone for that were out of my control.

"No sad talk today. All right? Let's just have a nice visit together. I baked some new cookies. Come, we'll sit in the living room and enjoy each other's company for awhile. Maybe this time you'll do the talking and tell me about your family and what you're studying in school."

The velvet sofa tickled my legs. I picked up one of the music boxes from the table and wound the key. Strains of Brahm's Lullaby relaxed me.

"I'd rather hear about your family. Tell me about Raizel and Lilya. Why don't you have any pictures of them?"

Minnie screamed. The iced tea she was holding fell from her hands. A wide stain spread across the sofa.

"My God, who are you? Now I know you must be a dybbuk who has come to end my days!" She gasped for air and tore at the collar of her dress, her eyes never leaving my face.

"Minnie!" I rushed to her side, but she pushed me away with a strength I didn't know she possessed and ran into her bedroom.

"Get out of here!" she screamed. "Don't ever come back!"

"I'm sorry about my temper this morning," Peter said. He put his briefcase on the chair and pulled me close.

"It was my fault," I answered. "I guess I have been a little crazy lately. But it's all over now."

He sat on his favorite chair and pulled me onto his lap. I rested my head against his chest, grateful that he was always extra nice after an outburst.

I wanted to tell him about all that happened that day, the child on the beach, my vivid memories, but then I would have to tell him about Minnie and I didn't dare risk his fury again. I snuggled closer, enjoying his smell.

"Who knows?" he said, as if reading my thoughts. "Maybe there is such a thing as reincarnation. Maybe there's more to this life than we know. One thing's for sure, if I come back, I want it to be with you."

Later that night, I crept out of bed, my body still warm from his kisses. I waited to hear Peter's snores, then walked into the living room.

It was a beautiful clear night. The moon looked bright through the open verticals. It was hard to believe the weather report that a hurricane hovered near our coast.

I lay down on the sofa. The leather felt cool against my body. I ran my hands through my hair and relived all that had happened that day.

A dybbuk, Minnie called me. A devil who came back to torment her. Maybe she was right. I probably was a devil. Maybe I deserved those beatings from my father and Peter. I would have to change my ways.

I woke to the smell of coffee brewing in the kitchen. Sun shone brightly through the patio doors. I rubbed sleep from my eyes.

"What are you doing up so early?" I asked. "This is unusual for you on Sunday."

"It looks like we're really going to get hit by the hurricane," Peter said. "I guess we won't be lucky this time."

I pointed to the bright sky. "Are you kidding? Look how clear it is out there. There's not a cloud in sight."

He laughed. "That's how much a woman knows. Stick to housekeeping. It's heading our way for sure and we're not even prepared." He opened the pantry door. "Damn it, you've been so crazy lately, you haven't even shopped. Come on, get your clothes on and we'll try to beat the mobs to the store."

The markets were chaotic. Shelves were almost empty, lines long, and nerves on edge.

I thought about Minnie. She would never be able to prepare for a hurricane. I should help her.

Then I remembered yesterday's visit. She never wanted to see me again. She called me a devil. Going there would be worse than staying away. Besides, Peter would kill me if he knew about her.

Whatever happened, she was no longer my concern. Hopefully, she would go to a shelter or ask one of her neighbors for help.

Hardly a breeze stirred as we prepared the house. We took in plants, taped windows and filled the tub and containers with water, but it still didn't seem possible that a hurricane would hit us. The sky still looked perfectly clear.

Late afternoon, it darkened. Palm trees swayed in

the growing wind. Loose papers floated in the air. I bit my nails as I watched weather reports on TV. This would be my first experience and I was frightened. My hands shook as I tried to prepare dinner.

Peter sat in front of the television set, a bottle of beer in his hands. I wondered what it would be like to be locked in the house with him if the electricity went off and he couldn't watch his programs.

Minnie's face flashed before me. She was alone, I was sure. Alone and terrified and I had failed her again.

The wind grew stronger. It lashed against the house and howled around the windows. Rain began to fall. The sky turned black. We held our breath as the electricity flickered and went off for a few seconds. Outside, there wasn't a sound of traffic. The only life we heard was the ever increasing volume of the storm and the weatherman's voice on TV.

"Damn it! We should have bought more batteries. We'll be lucky if we get through the night with what we have!" Peter shouted.

I moved close to him on the couch, staring ahead at the sliding doors, praying the tape would hold.

"We'll get storm doors and windows when this damn thing is over," Peter said.

We sat glued to the television as Hurricane

Andrew hit the Miami coast, gaining intensity, uprooting thick Banyan trees that had stood for years, smashing windows, lifting roofs.

With each blast of wind, I grew more frightened. My teeth chattered, perspiration covered the back of my neck. I wrapped my arms around Peter and prayed the storm would stop.

There was a loud crash against the front door; a pounding over and over. A relentless thump, thump, thump. The front windows broke, throwing glass all across the living room.

Peter shouted above the noise "Quick. Get as many towels as you can find. Blankets, anything!" We ran to soak up any onrushing rain, but fortunately, the force of the wind carried the rain away from the house.

I stared at the verticals dangling at the sliding door, metal slats hanging on broken cords. The blinds changed forms and became bearded, skull-capped men dangling from trees in the dark woods. Sounds of the storm changed to screams of victims. Heavy, marching boots were all around.

"Malke, Malke!" I ran for the door. "I've got to save her." I pulled at the knob, but the suction of the wind held it firm.

"What are you doing?" Peter shouted and pushed me back with such force, I slid across the tile floor, my knee scraping a vase that had fallen off a shelf. Blood oozed from the small cut.

"I can't let her down again. She's alone. I have to get to her!" Once more I ran for the door, my screams echoing off the walls. I felt as if I would go mad.

Peter's hand lashed against my cheek. I hardly felt it's sting. I was as out of control as the storm.

"Stop it!" His hands dug into my shoulders as he shook me. He carried me, screaming, kicking into the hallway and pinned me to the floor.

"What the hell are you talking about? Who the hell is this Malke creature that has you nuts?"

"I failed her once in Russia," I sobbed. "During the war. I can't let her down again."

Peter looked at me strangely. "What the hell kind of language are you speaking?"

I realized I had been speaking in Russian.

Suddenly, there was a loud pop. Our electricity was gone. Outside, the wind screamed and metal continued to bang against our door.

"Malke!" I shouted. "Malke, they're coming! They're coming! Hurry, you and Meyer get the girls and run!"

In the dim beam of the flashlight, Peter's face was strained, confused, angry.

"You've got to believe me, Peter. I was there. I lived before. I remember every detail. Please listen, or I'll go crazy.

A muscle near his mouth twitched. His eyes turned black and his arms tightened around me, pressing and squeezing my breath away.

"Tell me what the hell is going on. Who the devil are these people you're raving about?"

I told him about the letter that arrived by mistake and my compulsion to deliver it myself. I told him about the pictures on the wall, the hold they had and my probing into information about reincarnation. The muscle near his mouth tightened as I spoke, and his fingers cut into my back.

"Peter, I lived in Russia, near the Ukraine. Oh, Peter, if we were there I could take you right to the house we lived in. I see it so clearly, the house and the thick woods surrounding us. Malke was a childhood friend. We played together, we grew together. Her father was the town doctor. He was so good to everyone. He saved so many people. But it didn't matter. There was always the underlying hatred of the Jew. I heard it all my life and I couldn't understand it, but I never questioned it. When the war came, things got worse. Even my own parents, who owed so much to the doctor started saying terrible things. I kept quiet, so no one would call me a "Jew lover."

I stopped to catch my breath. The flashlight in Peter's hand was flickering, but the fury on his face was obvious. Soon, we would be in total darkness. The voice of the weatherman continued to come through the transistor radio on the floor. Shortly, that, too would be gone. We had no back-up batteries. It hardly mattered to me. I was no longer in Miami. I was in another world, another lifetime, and it was far more ominous than a mere hurricane.

My voice was low. I sensed the rage building in Peter, but there was no stopping my flow of words.

"It was near the end of September. We knew the Nazis were going to round up all the Jews. We knew they were going to be sent to death camps. Malke came and begged me to hide Raizel and Lilya, her two children. 'Hide them, please,' she said, 'you have a place on your loft. Meyer and I don't care for ourselves, but maybe you can save our girls.'

"I never forgot the look on her face when I refused. After all, I was afraid if they found out, they would kill me and my children. Not only did I refuse to hide them, but I turned them in to the Germans. The next day, the Nazis came and rounded up over 30,000 Jews and took them to the woods. They made them dig their own graves, then shot them in the head. Men, women and children, while the townspeople cheered and urged them on. I saw it, Peter. I was there. I saw it all. Please believe me."

All around us, in the darkened hall, Hurricane Andrew continued its destruction. Glass shattered, furniture shifted, a ceiling beam fell in the den.

Peter's voice rose above the sound of the storm. "I think you're nuts. I think you're out of your mind."

"I'm not nuts. I remember standing on the side with the others, watching, knowing I was responsible for the girls being there. Raizel and Lilya saw me. Their last words were, 'Ninotchka, help us!' before shots were fired into their brains. Blood ran all around the pit and the bodies were dumped into the graves like so much garbage while my neighbors cheered and I did nothing! Nothing! I will never forget, not if I live ten lifetimes. Now do you understand why I have to go to Malke? I can't let her down again. This is my Karma!"

Peter's lips curled downward. I hardly heard the words he hissed at me, but I knew the sound of an oncoming rage.

"You're out of your goddamned mind. I'd like to throw you out in the storm right now and let you die with your crazy ideas. This is the thanks I get for letting you live here and buying you a car and taking care of you. Karma! You must be *my* Karma!"

His hand reached out and hit my cheek. The blow

knocked me backward. "Maybe that will keep you quiet for awhile."

"I'm sorry. I'm sorry," I mumbled. I crawled into a corner of the room and curled up with my fist in my mouth.

I AWAKENED THE NEXT MORNING in the same position. Hurricane Andrew had moved out of our path and the sky was bright and clear.

Peter's curses came from the bedroom. "Get the hell in here and give me a hand with some of this crap!"

Furniture in the room lay broken, scattered all across the floor. The drapes had long slashes where the wind had torn through. Large pieces of glass lay across the bed, glittering under sunlight that shone through the splintered jalousies.

"Get this crap off the bed," he yelled. "Make yourself useful for a change!"

The glass shards pricked my fingers as I piled them into the trash can, but I bit my lips to keep from crying out. From the corner of my eye I watched Peter's every move. He tossed heavy sections of furniture out of the way as if they were toothpicks, the muscles in his arms bulging under his tee shirt, his hairy arms wet with sweat.

Blood squirted from my hand as a sharp piece of glass cut me. I let out a moan and put my hand in my mouth to suck the blood.

Peter's head shot up at my cry. His face looked twisted, his eyes turned black.

He was no longer Peter, the man I had been living with for more than a year. The tee shirt no longer read, "Miami Dolphins." It was the uniform of the Third Reich. The wood in his hand turned into a rifle and he was aiming it at the helpless Jews lined up in front of the graves they had dug with their bare hands. The townspeople were laughing and cheering him on. "Shoot! Shoot!" they yelled. And I was there, one of them, caught up in the hysteria of the mob, watching, encouraging as my friends and neighbors were being massacred.

Peter came toward me, the leg of a chair held high in his hand. I knew he could kill me with one swift blow and would do it without remorse. The soul of the Nazi still lived in him. His rage was more menacing than the fury of the hurricane.

I waited until he came closer, then pushed an ottoman in his path. The weapon in his hand fell as he landed on a pile of broken glass. He screamed as sharp points punctured his arms and legs. Blood squirted from the wounds.

I wanted to go to him, help him, but I knew he would strangle me with his bare hands.

A stream of curses followed me into the living

room. My purse sat in the middle of the room, its contents thrown all around the carpet. I had to get my keys before Peter gathered enough strength to follow me. They were in my hand when the force of his fist hit my back. He spun me around, ready to punch again, then lost his footing on water that had leaked in from the hole in the roof. He slid across the room, his head hitting a broken vase. He lay quietly and I thought he was dead, but I fought the urge to run to him. He was no longer Peter. Just an inhuman beast from a past life.

The front door hung on its hinges. I squirmed through the narrow opening and a beautiful, strong sunshine blinded me momentarily. I blinked my eyes, wondering if the last twenty four hours had been a figment of my imagination.

Large trees lay across the lawns, telephone wires hung lifelessly from poles and broken windows were scattered on the street. There was no longer a question in my mind about the hurricane or my own sanity.

My car stood in the driveway, its rear window cracked, paint scratched from fallen branches. I prayed the motor would start, that I could escape in case Peter came after me.

The ignition sputtered, then died. "Start, damn it, start," I pleaded. It sputtered again, then kicked over. I breathed in relief when I heard curses coming toward me.

The motor roared as I pushed my foot hard on the accelerator. The car skidded on the wet driveway, heading toward the garage. I pulled the wheel hard to the right with Peter hanging on to the door handle, screaming and cursing.

I pushed down harder and the car took off, leaving Peter sprawled in its wake. Now, if only I could reach Minnie in time.

My car inched its way through deep puddles and rubbish. Again, I marveled at the placid weather. "The calm after the storm" was an appropriate phrase.

Static on the radio cleared. The announcer urged everyone to keep calm, everything would be fine. Just keep away from Country Walk and Homestead. The destruction there was worse than anyplace else. No one was permitted in those areas.

Country Walk was where Minnie lived. I had to get to her one way or another and see if she was still alive.

Emergency wagons blocked the entrance to Country Walk. Shattered roof tiles, broken furniture, uprooted trees lay everywhere. The neighborhood looked like the Ukraine after the Nazi blood bath. I expected to see bodies strewn across lawns, hear the pounding of boots storming the streets.

I inched the car toward Minnie's street. A police officer barred the way. "Where do you think you're going? Nobody's allowed in there."

"Please," I pleaded. "My grandmother's in there and she has a bad heart. I don't know if she's dead or alive or if she needs help. Please let me through."

He must have sensed the urgency in my voice. "Okay, but you'll never be able to get the car through. Park here and walk carefully. There are lots of fallen wires. Let us know if you need help."

I stepped around piles of furniture and toilets and sinks lying broken on the street. I side-stepped live wires and tiptoed through high puddles.

Minnie's door was broken, but the mezuzzah, the religious metal she had explained to me remained firmly attached to the frame.

Inside, smashed dishes and furniture barred my way. The velvet sofa was covered with tiles from the fallen roof. Years ago, storm troopers had left ruins like this.

"Malke," I called, expecting to see her twisted, smashed body on the floor. "Malke."

I walked slowly from room to room, past the portraits still hanging securely on the walls, their eyes following my every move.

A moan came from the bedroom. Minnie lay on the floor, her leg pinned under a dresser drawer, her hand clutching a picture of two dark haired young girls with long braids.

"Don't try to move. I won't fail you this time." I said in Russian. She nodded and tried to smile.

With an effort, I lifted the drawer. Her leg was purple and swollen. "Can you get up?" I asked. She shook her head and moaned. Her face looked slate-gray, her breathing labored.

I tugged at her. "I'll try to lift you up."

Her eyes watered as she looked at me. "No. It's no use."

"Don't say that. I'll go for help. The man outside said I should call him if we need help."

She stroked my arm. "No, darling. I'm an old woman. I'm sick. I'm ready to go now to my family."

"I've failed you again," I said in Russian.

"You couldn't help it, Ninotchka," she whispered.

"You know? I'm not crazy? You believe it, too?"

Her voice was so low I could barely hear her answer. "Yes, I believe it. When I was a little girl, my father gave me a book about Cabala. I never forgot it. Like my father told me, knowledge never leaves you. I believe that a person's nashuma, their soul, can never die."

She closed her eyes and I was sure she was gone. I held her closer and kissed her forehead.

"Can you ever forgive me for not helping you?" I pleaded as I watched her draw her last breath.

Sirens wailed down the streets. I heard loud voices outside surveying the damage. Someone pounded on the walls. "Are you all right in there? Do you need help?" The officer I had spoken to earlier leaned down and looked at Minnie's body. "I'm sorry, Ma'am," he said. "We'll have someone come as soon as possible. Is there any other next of kin?"

I shook my head. "No one. Just me. I'll stay with her until someone comes."

For the first time since I had met her, Minnie looked at peace. Her mouth was no longer distorted, her face unlined, unworried. It was the face of the woman I knew a long time ago.

I held her a little longer, then walked into the hall. The pictures were alive again, friendlier, no longer accusatory. I went into the kitchen where the smell of Minnie's coffee and cakes still lingered. On the table were two letters. One was addressed to me and the other was the one I delivered to her such a short time ago. I picked that one up first and read the Russian words.

Dear Malke:

I went back to Russia. Back to where we used to live. Everything looked the same as it did before the war though nothing was really the same. I walked through the streets we played on as children and remembered when the Nazis came and everyone turned against us. Even Ninotchka who had been our friend for so long. The little shul was empty, but I saw our Rabbi standing at the pulpit. I heard his voice reciting the Shema before they dragged him by his beard and hung him from the tree. Malke, can we ever forget? I suppose we should, but it stays with me every day of my life. I'm sorry I walked those streets again. Sometimes it's better to let go of the past.

I will be going back to Israel soon to try to live out my last years in peace. Maybe someday you will visit me. After all, we are the only ones left of such a large family.

Shalom, my cousin.

Berta

I read the letter addressed to me.

"Dear Ninotchka:

How strange that my cousin's letter brought you back to me. My life is coming to an end. Soon, I will be with Meyer and the girls. Every day I see on television the people who say it never happened. They never saw what I saw. You, who were our friends and neighbors turned into maniacs when the Nazis came. "Kill the Jews" became the password. Even you, my dearest friend became an enemy and refused to hide the girls you once loved so much.

Meyer and I wanted to die with the girls and the rest of our people, but my cousin, Berta and her husband grabbed us and pulled us into the woods. Freedom Fighters found us and forced us to live.

"Some of us must live," they said. "We can't let them kill us all or no one will know what happened. We have to survive to let the world know."

Ninotchka, I pray that some day you will see what I have written and know that I forgive you at last. You were only one person caught up in the madness. You didn't have a choice.

Malke

I put the pad down, wiped my eyes and walked back into the bedroom. Minnie looked at peace lying on the floor.

"Malke, you're wrong. The day your girls died, I did have a choice, but I did nothing. I wonder if I will ever be able to let go of the past. Or will I bear this Karma forever?"